Never Fall in Love with a Vampire. It is a Pain in the Neck

By

Chris Crase

© 2001, 2002 by Chris Crase. All rights reserved.

No part of this book may be reproduced, stored in a retrieval system, or transmitted by any means, electronic, mechanical, photocopying, recording, or otherwise, without written permission from the author.

ISBN: 1-4033-3073-5 (Electronic)
ISBN: 1-4033-3074-3 (Softcover)
ISBN: 1-4033-3075-1 (Dustjacket)

This book is printed on acid free paper.

1stBooks - rev. 09/30/02

Never Fall in Love with a Vampire. It is a Pain in the Neck

Chapter 1

Christine did not think much of moving to L.A., home of the eccentric, strange, beautiful, freakish, plastic enhanced, and what not, being a 700 year old vampire. She would just assume her role as an uptown prostitute. Bar hopping on a nightly basis to find that young, horny buck. Some nights it would be rough but she could always find a willing boy at the local universities even though she loathed the frat parties, and she would avoid them all together if she had a choice. Of course, Christine could be a little less picky about her diet: young males in somewhat healthy shape but with a shy personality. Christine loves the idea of getting a nice, innocent male in her arms and succeeds about every other week. The others are just too easy of a prey for a woman, especially the woman who has had seven centuries to learn the little games of one night stands.

The other night she bagged a tasty 20-year-old kid. As tasty being, vampires can be just as particular about blood as you or I might find such fancies among wine. Still you will have the others who are quite satisfied with the brown bag routine. As for Christine one might call her a semi-enthusiast in the art of wine. She went to an all ages dance club down along the strip. For being 700 years old, Christine does not stop turning heads. One of the perks of being a vampire is the stoppage of time so Christine still had her shapely self of the age of 17 when she first met her friend Morgan.

She arrived at the dance club just after the sunset. She frequented many of the clubs to seduce the young men. The club she chose allotted itself with enough darkness and the typical set up of an overdone, underrated light show; it smelled of teenage drunk girls, cigarettes, and cologne from the men and boys whom will end up with the girls at the end of the night.

She entered the bar after talking the bouncer out of a cover charge. The center of the club had a pit set up for the dancing where one could enter under the watchful eye of the people surrounding the floor. They lingered on the stools and tables that were around. Christine made her way through the crowds that gathered in the most opportunistic places for voyeurism. She managed to only be patted by only a few hands, as most of the guys were not paying much attention to the girl making herself to the bar. The music was incredibly too loud which made all but yelling meaningless verse.

Christine sat up at the bar and ordered a favorite of hers. She scopes the club with her innocent gaze looking for young men standing against the wall. These are of course the shy ones. The shy guy who comes with friends and stands in the corner looking like he is enjoying himself while his friends dance, drink, grind, smoke, and enjoy their parade. The men who

Chris Crase

reluctantly look at a girl from across the bar hoping she will come over and talk to them and take them on the magic carpet ride, but at the end of the night they always walk the lonely sidewalks of Los Angeles. As Christine finishes her first survey of the bar, she identifies two prospective males at the far end of the club. Taking a sip of her drink, an older man in his late 20's surprises her at the bar. It never fails. Everywhere she goes she has to deal with them. Before she turns to him she bets herself. The guy will have a black leather jacket/slash overcoat; a button white shirt, top three unbuttoned; a gold necklace, probably with a cross; gel slick haircut; and sunglasses in his shirt pocket. Christine swivels to face him and is once again is proven wrong, the shirt is cream colored not even half and half quality. She smiles of course to be polite.

Five minutes later the man leaves after Christine has listened to his lines, second she enjoys playing the ditz, third she brushes his arm off her, fourth brushes his arm away again, and lastly (this lasts for 4 minutes and 35 seconds) she belittles every and any thing this man has to show for himself which by and by was not much.

Christine turns back to her drink and mutters, "It is tough to be kind to men sometimes," and proceeds to smirk.

Ordering another drink, she turns her attention back to the two boys against the wall. Damn her luck, one of them had left and the other is talking to a drunk girl, oh well the girl won't get very far with him she thinks. She will wait a little longer after all it is going to be a long night.

Never Fall in Love with a Vampire. It is a Pain in the Neck

Chapter 2

Christine glances down the bar and notices a man in his early twenties. I smile at her and motion to the guy she just shot down. She looks over to a table where she sees the man working a girl that is barely old enough for a driver's license. She shakes her head while turning back to me and I start to laugh at the situation. Christine begins to laugh with me and signals me over.

I picked up my beer and headed over to the stool next to her. "I cannot believe you are letting that little hussy take your man!"

Christine laughs again and introduces herself.

"I am Leif." I stated.

Christine looks over me with a careful eye. Not bad, she thinks but she already had her heart set on the other gent in the building.

"By looking at you Leif, I'd say you are new in town" Christine stated.

I look at the bar and then the crowd with a mused frustrated look and said "Do I look too much of a tourist, sort of a young lamb to the slaughter if you will." Looking around again I feel for the stool and slump onto it. "You are right though I arrived in town only yesterday off a freight train coming down from the north."

Christine lights up a smoke and blows it into my face, "Well I would not put it that way per say but you definitely do not fit into the L.A. scene. You are too normal for this town." She smiles and grabs her drink.

"Well if you are talking about all the vampires roaming through the valley, no I am not like that."

Christine chokes on her drink from the remark.

I looked rather surprised. "You cannot tell me that you have never heard that song before, Chris?"

"Oh no, it is just that I have never had anyone describe L.A. like that before, it just got me off guard."

"Being from Los Angeles, I would not think anything would be interpreted as off guard."

"It just hit a little too close to home. I mean you have been here all but 24 hours and have already figure out our little secret. So anyway Leif what are you doing in L.A?"

"To keep it interesting."

"To keep what interesting?"

"I move about when I get the grumble in the gut. So I got the pain and came out west. I figure it is my way."

Chris Crase

"Is it in your way to find yourself to these types of clubs. You don't exactly look like you belong here."

"Nah, as I said I just get into town so I am figuring this place out. Someone recommended a place down here on the strip and when I could not find it I came here."

"Oh, what was the place you were looking for?"

"Just a bar, I was looking very hard for it and gave up after night fell so I stopped in here for a beer before heading on."

"You got that grumble again, huh?"

"Hah, no just a need to find a different place than this, a much different place than this."

"Not into the vampire seen are ya?"

"Now you are fucking with me."

"Perhaps." Christine smiling.

I finished off the rest of my beer and proceeded to light up a smoke feeling the scene getting to me.

"Well Chris, I must be going I haven't any garlic, or crosses, and other trinkets to ward the L.A.ites off so I should get home early."

"It was nice meeting you, Leif" 'Now', Christine thinks, 'where is that boy gone too.'

I exit the club to search for a place that better suits my mood.

Chapter 3

Scanning the previous location of the boy, Christine assumes that he had left. She turns back to her drink and rethinks her strategy. Christine looks back at the slovenly drunk that approached her earlier and figures, "What the hell, I can deal with it for one night."

She gets up from her stool and adjusts her skirt and proceeds over to the to guy with his darling girl. She proceeds to smile as she struts the bar. Christine then glances over the man, she chose by default and sees the boy she was ever so interested in before coming from the rest room. Meanwhile, the man in his black leather jacket gets from his chair to meet Christine on the way. Christine ignores the guy as he says, "Change your mind sweetheart." and she proceeds to walk by him.

The boy was along the wall on the other side of the club. Christine bobbed and weaved the crowd. As she approached the kid the people seemed to crawl out of the woodwork to try and hamper her crossing. She caught the boy off guard as he was adjusting his shirt and checking his pants for wet spots.

"Hi, I am Christine."

The boy trying to keep his cool because he knows that some of his friends might just see him with this girl, "Hi, Christine? My name is Paul, so what is going on?"

"Well, I was wondering if you would like to dance?"

"Um, well sure I guess I can do that." Paul responded, starting to let his nervousness show.

"Great!" Christine takes his hand and leads him out to the dance floor as they start to grind on each other.

"God, why do the boys have to pretty much hump ones self when you just want to dance?" Christine thinks to herself. "Are they that desperate to cop a feel?"

Paul begins to let his hands roam. Christine knows that this is how guys act though. Show them a little attention and they are all over you.

"Oh well, it is better than having to cook and clean up after them," she thinks "but not by much." The dance floor was alive in a drunken orgy of males and females as the music blared over their heads. Bodies moved in and out of the space of Christine and Paul as the sweat gleamed off the lights. More and more people congested the already congested area as the people lost more and more inhibition and still the music played in excess. After about a hour of this, Christine figures it is time to move on to the next

Chris Crase

step besides her rump is starting to get bruised by Paul's excessive hip thrusts.

"Let's get out of here," she yells at him.

Paul nods his head and proceeds to lead Christine out of the dance floor. Paul looks back to make sure his friends who are standing at the fences of the floor see him leaving with Christine.

"How insecure." Christine almost feels sorry for this guy.

Passing the bar, Christine sees the guy with resistible moves on that girl's breasts and his tongue down her throat.

"I should come back for him later and take care of that asshole," She thinks. "Maybe I will depending on how long it takes to finish with this guy… Paul? I think."

Knowing that this guy probably rode with his buddies, Christine suggests that she drive. They get into her convertible roadster, which she loved, even though it was a typical girl car that usually is given to them by their father. In a flash they are off, Christine drives the town looking around for that nice secluded alley or parking lot that is dimly lit. Paul is rambling off about the college he is planning on attending and the majors he is considering and the times he gonna miss with his high school buddies jumping classes and the house parties and the…

"There it is, a nice little alley way that looks stripped of life." Christine says to herself. She pulls into the dark and proceeds down the dirt ridden back alley. Paul feeling the anticipation in his pants starts to squirm a little.

"Nervous?" Christine smiles to him as she turns off the lights and comes to a stop.

"Me, nah, I am just a little cold from being in the dance club sweating away and then have the wind blow it away, ya know."

"Well then… let me warm you up." Christine climbs on top of him as Paul reinitiates his aggressive behavior similar to his dance style. After about thirty seconds, Christine has had enough she starts to make her way down from his mouth. Starting with a lick to the ear, Christine moves her hands to Paul's shoulders. She licks it softly as Paul starts to pull up her skirt. Down the side of the neck edging ever so close to her meal, Christine continues her seduction. She learned of a neat little trick when sucking blood from a victim. A bite more to the front of the neck will puncture the windpipe disallowing the person to let out a scream.

With a swift lick of her red lips Christine takes a bite and forces her victim into a lapse. Paul tries to resist but Christine has more strength with every sip. A minute later Paul lies motionless; Christine pulls the handle and nudges Paul out of the seat into the alley with her heels. She hops out of her car and adjusts her dress a little. She pulls a knife from her glove

Never Fall in Love with a Vampire. It is a Pain in the Neck

compartment and proceeds to hide her calling card. She riffles the pockets takes out his wallet and throws it a couple feet away. Adding a couple of slashes around the body to make look like a struggle, she also drops a ten to make it look like a fast mugging. Driving down to the next street and turning onto the drag to head home, Christine pulls to a stoplight and glances into the rear view mirror and sees some blood on her chin. She pulls out a tissue and wipes it away as a group of guys pull up next to her. Hooting and a hollering at her, Christine thinks "Why not?"

Chris Crase

Chapter 4

I awoke that morning in my beat down apartment near the campus. Fumbling in my boxers, I plop down on my thirty dollar shag green couch and light up a cigarette. I hate mornings, so bright and cheerful for a man with a hang over. I make my way to the coffee pot through the mud thrown, war torn, smoke smelling, flower killing arena called my life. There is sitting a fresh pot of joe awaiting. Automatic timers are the greatest invention by man. Slapping the power button on the stereo, I proceed to sniff out the cleanest pair of jeans. To the washroom I go to cleanup the stubble of my chin, brush away the animal that died in my mouth and push down my mane. Retreating back to my couch, I light up another cigarette and drink my cup with joe.

"Almost out of synthetic cream; I got to pick up some more today. I wonder it this stuff is actually white or they make it that way. It would be cool if is was blue and turned my coffee a really ugly color."

I open the front door and am blown back by the intense sun flares. I am being punished, I know it. I grab the paper from my step. Lucky for me the last tenant forgot to cancel the subscription. I leave the door open to air out the bar fumes. Sacking out on the couch for the next hour, I throw my forearm over my eyes as I let out a scream like that of a witch being drenched in soap water.

"Why must the joys of life come with such pain. What god would give us such tools of pleasure and extract his own amusement ten fold form it?" Cursing my state of being.

I peruse the daily news and laugh at some of the articles that plague the newspapers. Drinking the coffee, it covers my upper lip rejuvenating my heart.

I find a T-shirt and throw on some shoes and head to the office of the registrar at the college. I wonder, "Who is the registrar is anyway. I never met the one at my other school; they probably don't exists." Reaching the registrar, the classes are filled out according to my regimen; I choose no class before noon. The line of a million patrons to get approved for learning awaits my arrival as another sign of the karma of excessive drinking. The guy in front of me is suffering from a heavy night of partying too. I strike up a conversation with him. He is not very receptive. What seemed forever in the California sun, I finally get inside to air conditioned building. Another 45 minutes later I am in front of a lady at one of the many computers in the room. She takes my card and punches in the three digit codes for each class.

Never Fall in Love with a Vampire. It is a Pain in the Neck

"That is it? Geeze they need to learn to automate." I mutter to myself.

The cashier is the next stop on my adventure yet in another building across campus. They line is not bad here. I walk up to the man in the window, greeting him and telling him I need to pay tuition. Rattling off my social security so he can retrieve my bill, I whip out a wad of money when he explains that he cannot take cash just credit, checks, or money orders. I walk away frustrated. I guess I will come back tomorrow.

After my treacherous tour of the college underbelly, I decide to continue my day out and about and make my way down to the local college businesses near the campus. "Bars, shirt shops, come on where is it, another bar, pizza joints, bong shop, shirt shop, copy place, bagalette, ah the coffee shop."

Strolling into the opened barrio, ordering a cup of joe, I find a little table in a sunlit corner. The college kid looks at me weird. I throw down my pack at the table, light up a smoke, pull out my next read, spill a little coffee on it as the cup misses my mouth.

I get interrupted by two girls that sit next to me. I eagerly engage in a conversation. They were freshmen and just got in the day before. One of them, Harriet, cute, was talking about her cheerleading days at some high school in Texas. The other, Michelle was interesting she was talking about her major in writing. It was an enjoyment seeing two fresh minds with no idea of the magnitude of adventure awaiting for them. So wide-eyed and careless. I wish I had that back sometimes, then again, I had it at least once a long time ago. We talked laughed flirted drank more coffee, went to the bathroom, got a caffeine buzz. Eventually they left to make their dinner call at the dining halls. I decided to call it quits as well as dusk was quickly approaching. I packed up and walk back home stopping for a slice of pizza and a couple of packs of smokes. Taking the long route home though I had no desire to quicken my destruction tonight.

Whereupon returning to my scuffle little abode, I showered before engaging in a night of meaningless drinking. I did, however, put on my same clothes. A little deodorant and some toothpaste and I am as good as new. Well, okay, new is not quite the case. The years have plague this weathered body. I remember when my little belly was a flat stomach. Skin smooth before the wind, ice, water, age, and puberty hit. The scars from childish games remain as well as the tattoos. Eyes kinder with wisdom have lost their sparkle of a kid's wonderment. Muscles get sore, when did that start? I never was sore as a whippersnapper running around. Through it all at least I can still dream and once in awhile I can feel those embers glowing inside me from past lives.

Chris Crase

I sit down and pick up my book to read for awhile before heading out. Fighting the urge of my body for a nap, I lose. Awaking from the thousand year slumber, I taste the muggy from the salt air. I hang my clothes on the deck as I shower quickly again and head out to conquer the rising night. The streets I walk are not new to me for the most part for I have a usual line of attack at which place to and not to hit. The first bar, five buck cover no thanks; the next is a blues club with a pretty good sound. I sit at the bar and suck down some tunes and a few suds and cigs. Off again, blocks away from my first stop I feel like I have entered an entirely new world. Streets seem safer; people look important, streetlights are crisp in design and function. I think I will stay a rub some shoulders with the social elite. I find a bar that looks just a little more up beat with the sounds of live piano. Maybe they will let me loosen up my fingers a little. I have not practiced in weeks, but why not.

Never Fall in Love with a Vampire. It is a Pain in the Neck

Chapter 5

At her apartment, Christine begins to make herself over for the night. Stepping out of the shower she thinks to herself what is she in the mood for tonight. "I think I want a college grad tonight, someone you has just started to make some money and lets people know it." She smiles to herself in the mirror as she applies her makeup to look like a working woman out to meet up with her friends. Over the years Christine has become quite astute of creating the right kind of bait for her catch of the night. She goes to her closet and finds her red dress. Professional yet the dress propels a nice sensual mystery about it. Christine thinks, "This is perfect for the piano bar". After applying some quick fixes to her hair at her hallway mirror she is off to wine and dine on her yuppie tonight.

As Christine pulls up to the bar, a young man hops to attention and adjusts his valet vest. She gives him the keys with a note, which read "I want to take you home with me tonight." Christine always does this to avoid tipping the valets. She thinks its cruel to get the boys hopes up but then again a dollar does not go as far as it did fifty years ago. Christine struts into the bar to the live piano music. She makes it a point to stress her walk to make every man and his girlfriend in the place notice her. Hopping up on the barstool, the bartender brings her a glass of Riesling.

"I did not order this." Christine states.

The bartender with a devilish grin says, "The two gentlemen at the end of the bar."

Christine looks over and sees to men smiling at her. She thinks to herself as she nods in appreciation, "This is going to easier than I thought" One of the men shoves an elbow into his friend indicating to make his move. Wincing in a little pain, the taller of the two gents makes his way over to Christine's space as the other watches on attentively.

"Thank you for the wine."

"It was my buddies idea."

"Oh?"

"Yes, well I just recently graduated from college from the Midwest and had to leave a good relationship out there as well. So, my friend is trying to get me back out in the scene."

"He must be a good friend."

"The best."

Christine glances to his friend who is watching with a shit-kicking grin on his face.

"So, why is a beautiful girl sitting here by herself."

Chris Crase

Christine thinks "Typical line he just turned me off." She looks at the questioner.

"I am suppose to be meeting some girlfriends, but I do believe I have been stood up."

"Well then why don't we get a table and enjoy the music. The guy who is playing now came in pretty much off the street and kicked the regular guy off. No one is complaining though because he is quite good."

"Sure why not" Christine jumps off the stool and her company leads her to a small black table. As the gent helps her into her seat she says "By and by my name in Christine."

"Oh how thoughtless of me, I am Chet and my friend at the bar is Buck."

"Please to meet you Chet."

"So what to you think of the piano player?"

Christine glances up from the table and looks over to the musician.

"Oh wow!! I know that guy."

"Who is he."

"Well I shouldn't say that I know him but I met him a couple of weeks ago at this dive on the strip" as Christine watches Leif play the piano with a look of flustered amazement.

"He does look like you would find him on the strip, wouldn't you say?"

"What do mean by that Chet." Christine still looking at Leif while his fingers danced across the Ivory.

"Well look at him, he seems like the guy who would hang out at those strips preying upon underage drunk girls."

"I really would not say he fits into those places well."

"Well he is not the type to visit these places either."

"Even though he may not be conducive to the scene, he seems to mold the scene around him to his own liking."

"How do you mean?"

"Okay, look at him: kinda scraggly and beaten down. He does not look like the person who is well adjusted at first glance. But a careful eye shows that he quite possibly just comfortable with himself as is. We should be the ones second guessing ourselves cause are not we the ones wearing the facades?"

"All I know is that this is me and I am wearing it. It is called success and I enjoy the company that it keeps. I personally would not want to surround myself with his type even if he is quick with his fingers. I would much rather be hanging around our kind."

"Well then, you will have to excuse me."

"Why?"

Never Fall in Love with a Vampire. It is a Pain in the Neck

"Is it not apparent? I am not one of your kind." Christine gets up and moves to the bar counter.

"Bartender, beer please."

She looks back toward the piano and sees Chet explaining to Buck what just transpired. She could tell Buck was saying forget it there are others around and begins to direct Chet to a table of three college ladies. The bartender brings the drink over to Christine. She turns to the barkeep and thanks him.

"Excuse me..." as the barkeep walks away, "I would like to buy one of these for the man at the piano. The bartender confused because he saw her and the other guy together moments ago shrugs his shoulders and waves a waitress over. Nervously she eyes the bartender making the drink and giving it to the waitress. It seems that time has practically stood still. The waitress leaves for the piano. Christine just stares at the back wall of the bar. Her back turned to the piano player she tries to look comfortable wondering how long it takes for the man to come over her. The music stops, her heart leaps into her throat, clapping assumes the prominent noise.

Christine thinks to herself "What the hell am I doing? I haven't acted this way over a guy, a guy I only met once especially, for ages. I should be in control of the situation. I am acting like an idiot! I should have never..."

"Chris is that you?" I said.

"Oh, hello Leif" As Christine turns to face me. "And it is Christine."

"Yea, I know but I prefer Chris."

"Oh,"

"I must say a red beer is not really my forte, but thank you anyway."

"Don't mention it, I thought you deserve someone to buy you a drink after that wonderful display of piano playing."

"Oh, I just dabble in it."

"For dabbling you sounded marvelous."

"You did not hear a single song I played did you Chris?"

Flustered now, Christine says "Why do you say that?"

"Anyone who gives me that much praise for playing must not have been really paying attention."

"Well, you are right." She smiles "I was trying to be..."

"Polite? Ah every one says that!" I smile "It doesn't bother me I just enjoy playing, I don't need the fame, accolades, or whatever with it. Just the play."

With that I look long into her eyes, she returns my gaze only for a moment before she seems to get a little edgy. She begins to look past my right ear and then returns to my stare. Again she does it. This is driving me

Chris Crase

insane; Chris looks so cute for lack of a better word I think to myself. Once again she looks away. I move my head closer to her.

"So, would you like to get something to eat." I say breaking the gaze into her soul.

"I guess so, I mean I was going to meet some friends, but never mind. Yes."

"Lets get out of here."

I throw down a twenty to the bar and help Chris out of the chair. I motion for her to lead as I follow. My eyes gaze over the crowd to see the men and women that I pleased for a short time. My eyes stop at two gentlemen, one of which is glaring intently at me. "Funny, usually every one enjoys my piano." I think to myself. We approach the front doors.

"Your car or mine?" Christine asks.

"Actually I walked here."

"Oh, then I guess it is mine."

Christine gives the ticket to the young lad who retrieves her car.

"Give the keys to him won't ya." Christine motions the valet as she proceeds into the passenger seat of her car.

The boy walks over to me and harshly slaps the keys into my hand with a look of anger and frustration on his face. I climb into the car and slowly pull away.

"That valet seems to be a little rude especially for a job that survives on tips."

"Oh, you know young men, he is probably sexually frustrated." Christine smirks. "Where are we going anyway?"

"I enjoy this seafood place down on the beach." Stopping at a light and fidget for a smoke. "It is a little run down but the atmosphere and the people are great. I have known the owners since I have been in L.A."

"Speaking of which, I know I asked you this before but, how long have you lived here?"

"Ahh, let's see… Tomorrow will be three weeks."

"Now, that is a long time" Exchanging smart ass smiles "Business trip?"

"Nah, I am changing careers and I moved out here to attend med school."

"Really? And what did you do before deciding to become a doctor?"

"I was a owner of a coffee shop in a small town on the coast North of Boston."

"Huh, how does one decide to go from a small business owner of coffee and cigarettes to becoming a family practice or whatever kind of doctor you are gonna be?"

Never Fall in Love with a Vampire. It is a Pain in the Neck

"Well, I can't sit stationary for a long time so I jump around a lot and this time it landed me here."

"So I take it you have not been a coffee entrepreneur all this time either?

"Nope, three years ago I was a thespian, in Montreal."

"And before your acting bug?"

"Ahh, you want all my secrets and past lives live now, then what would be left to talk about tomorrow?"

"You seem, pretty confident of a second date, what makes you think I will go out again with you."

"Well if I tell you all my secrets now then there won't be as good of an opportunity for another date. I am just playing the odds."

"Are you good at gambling?"

"Actually I just lost $1000.00 bones at Vegas a week ago. Damn those spinning wheels thingies."

"So why are you playing the odds that I will go out again?"

"You know what they say, you cannot teach an old dog new tricks."

"I bet I can get you to roll over."

"What kinda of odds you giving me?"

"Not good."

"That is just the way I like it."

Arriving at the beach, Chris and I enter the restaurant whereupon we were greeted buy a waitress. I asked for a table on the deck out looking the ocean. I love the breeze, so many things we take for granted such as the warm flowing air around us in a calmly night. I look out across the ocean; so many years since I made my way across the sea. Still I find myself longing for that openness and freedom of the ominous blue. I rest my elbow on the rail and lean out over the edge of my seat. Hoping, wishing a breeze will swipe me from the bounds of this world. Lift me up over the waves, mystify me with your sweat Poseidon. Sirens sing to me I will answer. Moon, hold me with your light above the waters guide me with your movement.

"Leif?"

"Oh, I do apologize I guess I was day dreaming. Then again I guess it isn't day dreaming since it is night so it must be lost in thought."

"About what?"

"Oh, about the beauty of the Pacific and how wonderful it would be to be on a magic carpet just above the sea line. Feeling the warm salt water on your finger tips."

Of all the years being a vampire Christine never had thought about using her talent of Icarus as nothing more than a mode of transportation. Now lost in thought of herself, Chris thinks of the last time she took a flight for pure

Chris Crase

enjoyment of it. It must have been a couple days after becoming the dead. One night in January, she remembers waking from her slumber and approached the window of her father's house as he did not know of her rebirth and she herself a little horrified of it as well. Opening the sill she glided out of window and proceeded along the tree line of their small farm. Christine remembers that night because she got her robe on a tree and was cursing herself for being so negligible.

"Chris? The waitress asked what you would like to drink?"

"Oh! Lets see, hmmm, how about a red?"

"I will take a red as well." I stated.

As the waitress retreats to the bartender Chris fumbles through her purse looking for her pack of cowboy killers. Puckering her lips as she looks at me, a casual flirting technique of hers.

"You know those things will kill you." I said while leaning back in my chair to reach for my own pack.

Chris just smiles as she thinks to herself, "Yes they do but too bad I am already dead."

"You should heed your own words Leif." Christine leans forward to receive a light from me.

"I know but I cannot help to think that I look so much cooler when I smoke." lighting my own. "So, Chris what is it that you do?"

"I am in advertising."

"Really, where do you work?"

"At home, I have landed some contracts that one could consider very stable and long term."

"Good for you, how did you do that."

"I slept with the management."

I proceed to choke on my wine as I look into a plain face of Christine trying to catch a glimpse that she is just pulling my proverbial leg.

"Well, I guess that is one way to do it."

"For getting what you want it is."

"Is that your approach on life then as well?"

"Well, yes I mean you men are so predictable and I can pretty much pick and choose from the lot."

"So you are basically treating us like cattle or a new car or"

"Well look at your species, Leif, from what I have experienced you guys only think about one thing. Everything you do is just presenting yourself better and better for your supposed next conquest. You go to school not for the education, you get a job not because you like it, haircuts, clothes, cars. Everything you men do is to try and get in a woman's pants. So if you guys are so vain then why should I not exploit it?"

Never Fall in Love with a Vampire. It is a Pain in the Neck

"I seem to have touched a chord with you and men."

"No, I just know the game and can play it."

"Ah, the game."

"Yes the game."

"I can appreciate a person who knows what they want and proceeds to get it by any means necessary. As long as they can accept the consequences of what becomes of it. That is pretty much my philosophy except I don't sleep with the bosses, not that I wouldn't if it help. It is just look at me. I think I would get fired if I did that due to lack of quality assurance. As far as the little game we mentioned that is something I cannot do. I do not know whether I lack the skills or the desire but more and more I think it to be desire. I just want to go out there and play if you will the bigger game of life before it shuts me down for good. I figure I will be dead by thirty so I best make the best of it before I am gone."

"I know what you mean about the desire to play the games, I really would rather not but since it is something this world expects and I have the skills why not, especially sense it is the only way for a women to get ahead in life."

"Ever try to play it straight?"

"Nah, I have seen what has happened to other women in my life, it is embarrassing to see them get screwed by the glass ceiling so I figure why not do the screwing get what I want and get out."

"Cannot argue with that line of thinking I guess, are you that determined to make it in the world?"

"That is an interesting thought, I really do not know, I guess it is something that I has been instilled in me."

"You see that is the key, we must first realize if we want to make it in this world or not. As I go I really do not care as you have heard I just do what I want."

"Easy for a male to say."

"Let's change the subject, eh."

"Why?"

"Because I can see this conversation getting really out of context and ugly really fast, besides our food has been here for the last five minutes." Christine glances down with amazement, "And I hate for it to get anymore colder."

Flustered, Christine begins her meal as I just kinda smirk and proceed to finish my cigarette. Dinner lasted all about ten minutes with the usual dinner conversation: How is yours, do you want to try a little, I need another drink, care for dessert?

Chris Crase

After eating, Christine lit another cigarette and watched as I excused myself to the "little boys room" as I stated so eloquently. Christine begins to think to herself, "Either Leif is the most annoying man I have met or I am starting to like him. Oh, come on girl, I am 700 years old, and I have met every kind of man. Why should he be any different. He's annoying, that is it and nothing more." Christine begins to grin. "Then again he has a certain charming thing about him, maybe I should hang around him a little longer before I decide to take his blood. Besides if he is just a pompous, bothersome, egomaniac, gross, obtuse, cocky, asshole, smelling pervert; I sure don't want that stuff running in my veins."

"Helllllooo?"

Christine turns to see me standing.

"Chris are you like comatose or something I have been trying to get your attention. I paid our bill do you want to take a walk on the sand?"

"Oh, ah… I can't I should be getting out of here and back home." Christine remembers that she still has to feed tonight and needs to find some lucky boy for that.

"All right then, let me give you my number and you can call me."

"Great, I will do that."

"Actually come to think of it I do not have a number, I have not set that service up for me but I am starting up school next week and I should be listed in the campus phone system."

"Argh, that is too complicated, here is my apartment number, give me a call tomorrow night and we will go and find something to do."

"Sure, I can do that, say around seven."

"Make it later."

"OK, then I will call tomorrow at dusk."

"Good. good night Leif, oh don't you need a ride back to that bar?"

"Nah, I am gonna stick around here and have a drink with the owner he can give me a ride."

"Are you sure?"

"Yep, no need to worry about me, I am a creature of the night and I can handle myself."

"All right, good night and thanks for dinner."

"Night, Chris."

"That is what I mean by annoying," Christine thinks to herself as she walks.

I smirk thinking to myself, "Man calling her Chris gets under her skin."

Christine drives off as I watch from the patio. "Well, Charlie," The owner of the bar grill looks over, "I struck out again, load me up." Charlie laughs and pours me another beer as I head to the stools in front of him.

Never Fall in Love with a Vampire. It is a Pain in the Neck

"Leif, haven't I taught you anything, you got to be a jerk to get anywhere with women."

I laugh "Oh man, Charlie I try but I just plain and simple bleed nice guy chump."

Charlie shakes his head in a sarcastic disgust.

"Besides Charlie, there is something different about this one that I can't quite grasp."

"So ya gonna see her again then eh Leifer?"

"Got a date tomorrow night."

"Well, then nothing to do till then except be merry and drunk."

"My point exactly Charlie."

I get up and walk over to the jukebox and throw a five in and put in the usual bar songs.

"Hey, Charlie." I shout. "Have I ever told you my theory about jukeboxes in the bars across the country, if you look at the selections they are pretty much the same. I mean of course you have the few new pop forty CD's that get changed out every month but for the most part you have your old staple collection. For instance you have the romantic love stuff so when those two drunk people are getting that drunk frisky feeling and are gonna end up at one of their places song, the my boy slash girl friend just dumped on me and I saw him slash her out at another bar with someone else song, the lets get cheesy and reminisce about our youth in the eighties which always seems to be good when we look back songs, and then the classic we are just getting drunk songs."

I sit back down.

"Well, Leifer had never thought of it that way, eh do you want me to change around the entire box?"

"And unbalance the entire universe! Heck no! This is probably the one true constant in nature, we could possibly send the entire world into upheaval if we did that."

"True, true, we better not play with the unknown forces in the world, eh Leifer?"

"I do not know Charlie, women are unknown forces as well and we keep messing around with them." as I light a smoke, "Speaking of theories, Charlie I have a theory about empty beer glasses."

By this time a young gent at the end of the bar was laughing his ass off. I look down to better situate myself for what look like another night of bar talk. He is about my age with a very skinny build and pale white skin and long black straight hair.

"Hey," I said rather boldly "What are you laughing at longhair?" A somewhat standard greeting among us dissidents.

Chris Crase

He comes over and sits down next to me and orders another beer. "How are ya doing?" he says.

"Good, except for the lousy service here."

Charlie grins as he starts to pour more beer for me and gives me the finger. Laughter ensues.

"Looks from what I saw that sweet little filly played you for a dinner and some drinks."

"Yeah, you are telling me," I turn my back to him, "Can you take that knife out of my back since you are sitting there."

"Hah, no problem man."

"So what is your story?"

"Same story, different bar."

"I hear that my friend, cheers."

"Cheers!"

Wiping the foam from my mouth I extend the same hand, "The name is Leif."

"Leif? How are you the name is Jarred."

"Jarred..." feeling the effects of the beer "I like you; you are a good soul."

"Thank you my friend so what happened with your lady friend? That is if you don't mind me asking."

"Actually I was playing coy with you earlier, I have a another date with her tomorrow." I pull out the piece of paper with Chris' number on it.

Jarred looks at the number and name, "Ah, I knew a girl named Christine once, she broke my heart."

"I will keep that in mind, Jarred, never trust a woman named Christine."

"Never trust any woman."

"You sound like myself, let me guess. You are one of the types where you get into a relationship and everything is going swell and then the next time you turn around... boom! A surprised uppercut that leaves ya bleeding for months until the next boxer get you in the ring?"

"Are my bruises that evident?"

"Takes an underdog to know an underdog."

"I will drink to that. So Leif, have you known her long?"

"Nah, this is just the second time I have seen her. The first time I met her we were at this other bar and some asshole dressed like the slick outfit type of guy tried to hit on her and she continued to reduce that jackass to a little pup whining for too be let outside."

"Sure a shame that guys like that usually end up with a chick at the end of the night anyway."

Never Fall in Love with a Vampire. It is a Pain in the Neck

"He did in fact, what the hell is up with that? Anyway, I admired Chris' approach to the situation and I guess you could kind of say that we hit it off."

"Excellent, my friend, well here is to a possible future of all nighters"

"I will drink to that, by and by what happened between you and you lady friend that was named Christine as well?"

"Bad blood, my friend, bad blood."

"Say no more, I hear ya."

Songs were played, lives of exaggeration told, alcohol consumed, smokes smoked, and women, well women suffered no mercy in our boisterous stories of past ex's. Charlie eventually kicked us out almost falling down the stairs himself. I guess that last call was his wife. Jarred had managed to relieve Charlie of a bottle of cheap rum. Naturally we could not taste the wretchedness of the swill as we drank it on the beach looking at the stars speaking proudly of our dreams. Jarred had come to L.A. with the same bag of tricks that most kids our age do: hope of selling a screenplay and retiring in that good part of California... where ever that is.

I woke the next morning with a pool of wet sand in my mouth which actually made it taste a little better. I stumbled around for my shoes as the morning sun made me seep the alcohol from my skin. Jarred was gone. To my chagrin he wrote a thanks for the hang over in the sand next me. Of course in my slumber and drunken, confused morning state I managed to erase part of the message. It read something like "Than f hun gover". I made my back to Charlie's where he was just pulling up and opening the restaurant. Charlie is a good man. He let me in and cooked me some breakfast with a lot of coffee as I cleaned up as much as I could.

"Ya know Leifer, for a person who is starting med school, the way you look I would never want to be sick again."

"I don't blame you Charlie, but I just want to get the degree. I will probably never use it."

"Huh, don't docs make good money anymore?"

"Sure they do I just want to see if I can get through it, and more than likely at the end of school I will be bored and go and do something else."

"You are one weird person Leifer."

"Charlie, my friend, you have no idea."

Chapter 6

Christine awoke just as the last beam of sun touch the ocean. Actually Christine has a bad habit of waking up before the sun sets. It started a few decades ago for no good reason. So, she just lays in bed listening to the outside world go about their lives. One of her fondest memories was when she was in up state New York in the fifties. The house next to hers had a child who was always called home as the sunset for dinner. She can still hear the girls swing set in her mind as it stood there swinging to a stop while the girl retreated into the house.

Startled by the phone, Christine realizes that the sun has said goodnight. She races from her room to the phone in the kitchen.

"Hello?"

"Hey, Chris are ya ready?"

"Oh, hey Leif, ah shit can you give me a half hour?"

"No!"

"…Excuse me?"

"Geeze, how come I am the only one that thinks that is funny?"

"Oh, ha, ha."

"Oooh, a little bit of sarcasm in your sweet voice I think I detect."

"Anyway Leif meet me at the bar with the piano in a half a hour."

"Actually that place really ain't my style but there is a small cafe two blocks north of there next to the bus station?"

"Okay that sounds fine, see you there."

"Later, alligator."

"Bye."

Christine hangs up thinking "Annoying." She scrambles about her apartment getting ready commonly known to women as the 15 minute drill. Over the years Christine has perfected it to seven minutes. Walking by the mirror at the door she stops to make any last second adjustments. "None needed," she smirks, "Haven't lost a step." And out the door she went to whatever that place was.

Christine pulls up to the cafe which literally looks like a bus that was going to pull out from the station but never quite made it. "Oh, I over dressed for this place." She spots me in the corner table smoking a cig and reading a book. She gets out of the car and strolls up to me as a thousand eyes from traveling people fall onto her.

"You obviously do not know one thing about impressing a lady."

"Wait to you try the coffee then I think you will owe me an apology," as I set down my book and motion to the waitress, "besides I have yet to determine if you are a lady." Christine gives me a smile of okay good one as she sits across from me.

She glances around the cafe: tables that seat four along the window, behind them are the stools that seem to extend forever down the counter, behind that the counter filled with soda fountains and small refrigerators to house the pies, salads, boxes of milk, behind that the kitchen with a cook and a dishwasher. The whole place covered in bright stainless steel bus siding covered a little by black and white pictures of the family and their friends that have run the place through the years. The stools and benches covered in that cheesy old red sparkling covering that has lost it sparkle over the years. She feels the loose end of some duct tape used to cover a tear stick against her cleanly shaven leg. A pinball machine stands next to us that hasn't been played for a decade and the soft tunes of a older jukebox plays in the smoke filled air of the cafe. The waitress approaches and refills the one cup of joe and she orders one as well, she leaves behind a pie menu.

"Well I will say this for the place, it has character. What type of character I have no idea."

Laughing "I am still trying to figure that out too but man… just look at the people. Here you have it a entire cross section of society: the well to do college kids who take the bus home to feel non-guilty about there wealth and there roommates lack of, the old who are going to see there children and ride the roads cause they trusted social security and their kids are too cheap to fly them, yet they go, the newly separated wives leaving the troubled lives behind, hopefully, the homeless with just enough money for a buck ninety-nine breakfast, served anytime, runaways, vagrants, kids wanting to see the country, military folk; I mean here it is… all different pasts all different hopes and dreams of something better. It is amazing!"

"So I see you are reading the Koran."

"Yeah, good stuff."

"Are you a Muslim?"

"On the contrary, I am an atheist."

"You don't believe in a god? Why?"

"I have no need for it."

"Oh that is interesting."

"So what is your opinion on the subject?"

"I guess like you I have no need for it nor anytime to think about it."

"Yeah, I just like to read about to figure out what draws people toward religion."

"So what do you think it is? By and by, you are right this coffee is good!"

Chris Crase

"You know I have been asking that question for the better part of three years or even since the day of inception. I really do not know; I think for some people it is a sense of belonging to something greater than themselves you know like a social club. Still for others I think they are just brought up in it with no real desire to question it. But it is the others that I am interested in the ones that see something there inherent. That something behind the picture or façade of the religions and what is the underlining meaning of it all. Those brave souls that go searching in something and come out fulfilled even more so than those that sit next to them at the pulpit. Their alms are something more which is interesting to myself that have had no such need, want, or desire. What is that? I know not many have it, still the ones that do it is something spectacularly alien."

"Perhaps it is their contentment and nothing more, a piece of mind or comfort they need to feel in this tipsy tervy world."

"Now that is an interesting point. Does it go any further than that? Does it need to go?"

"I do not know, these people you refer to have gone to hell and back and then to heaven and back examining their own belief's, other's, questioning everything written and beaten it up as well as themselves. Maybe they arrived at what they believe a god could be beyond the Bibles, Korans, Torahs, writings, and what have you to concept indifferent of those to a basic idea maybe."

"Huh, I have to think about this, but for another time. Do you want to get out of here and go for a walk?"

"Yes, lets do that."

As we exited the cafe and walk along crack asphalt, I said, "By and by, I meant to tell you that you look… well incredible tonight."

"Thank you Leif, I spent a hour trying to find the shoes for this dress."

"That is why I like being a guy, the most pair of shoes I owned at one time in my life is three: sneakers, deck shoes, and work boots. That is all we have to have."

"That is why I like being a woman, all the pairs of shoes I own were bought by guys like you."

"You got me on that one, but I never bought a shoe for a woman and never will."

"I will take that as a challenge."

"Go ahead, but I will not lose; I will buy you everything else in the world if I have too but… nope you will never get shoes from me."

"Somehow I get the feeling you are right Leif."

We strolled down the avenues just like James Dean, no worries, no cares, no fears. We passed buildings both old and new and I just babbled about them to Chris. The reason I like this one as compared to that one. How the stone of this wall is better cause of textured properties or how bricklayers lay down bricks on a wall in a certain way to make it appear that we perceive objects in them. The facade of this one where that one is obvious a bank cause one can tell it was made for functionality and bottom dollar. Of course I talk out of my ass a lot, but in the end somehow I get a better appreciation for it all. And then I caught the reflection of the moon battling city lights in the face of a glass building.

"The moon will be full soon, I say another week, ah I love the moon. I mean geeze those lucky bastards thirty years ago got to take the ultimate road trip. Keroauc eat your heart out."

Chris glances up to the moon from its reflection and says, "Leif have you ever been in at the edge of the Rockies to the east and seen that magnificent ball of cheese rise up in the summer and you swear that it was dipped in blood?"

"No, but I have heard. I will see some day."

"Someday… Hey have you ever howled at the moon?"

"Sure, I am usually drunk but every now and again I have been known to do such, how about you?"

"No." Christine chuckles a little.

"Come on lets do it."

"No!"

"What are you afraid of making a idiot of yourself."

"Yes."

"Then that is why exactly it must be done."

I give a little grin to Chris and then I arch my back and get a chest full of the night smog and say to her, "Follow my lead."

And then I let it all out as people a block away pick up their pace to get away as soon as possible. By the time I finish I have to shimmy step back to catch my balance and then I hear Chris try.

"Boy, that is bad," I said, "we are gonna have to work on that come on lets give it another shot."

I took her hand and continued to walk and howl amid conversation of hopeless dreams. If you had a million dollars and which movie star would you want a conversation with. By the time we got back to the car it was three. The streets were now empty and the last bus full of people departed for another world and she stood there by the side of her car as I sat on the hood finishing up the last part of our conversation.

"Well it is pretty late and I should retreat to my asylum, Chris."

"Yeah, I should be heading off too, I have work tomorrow."

"Oh man, you will be hating life tomorrow morning, eh?"

Chris Crase

"Nah, it is sometimes worth it."

"Now why did you have to go and say that. I was having a great time and for the past five minutes I have been trying to work up the nerve to kiss you and it almost seems that it is expected."

Christine smiles "I am sorry to put you in that situation but I had to compromise your situation so you would kiss me."

"So damn, I guess I have to do it. Of course you know now it is awkward and stuff and both of us are probably thinking I hope my mouth does not taste as bad as I imagine and I know we will both turn the same way and knock noses and…"

"Oh, shut up" Chris grabs the back of my neck and pulls her lips up to mine as I am instantly tasting raspberry lip gloss. It does not taste that bad. The kiss lasted all but ten seconds, well O.K. more like five. Christine got into her car a started to drive off waving her right hand as she watched me from the rear view mirror. At that moment I could only do one thing so I reared up with all my might and cut loose a howl that echoed down the streets breaking the nights hold on the silences. Then I heard Chris give a howl back in acknowledgment.

"Yep," I said out load, "just got kissed by a beautiful woman." I glance around, "And now one is around to verify it and now I am standing here having a conversation with myself."

I stuck my hands in my pockets, sunk in my shoulders, pivoted my right foot 90 degrees, leaned back and just let my toes lead into the humid night. I followed with a shit kicking grin and a little whistle going. Probably left as a gift from Chris.

Chapter 7

The next few weeks were the most fantastic and confusing experience I have had in my short lived life. My classes already took their toll on me; hardly any sleep these days, the only thing that kept me going was the intensity of classes, the cigarettes, coffee, more coffee, and Chris' smile. After two months, dry of alcohol, I yearned for my first free night. Chris already had plans, so I headed out with some classmates to the bars with delusions of drunkenness dancing in our heads. However, we had not one stinking person to volunteered themselves as a designated driver so we consented to a college bar within stumbling distance. The bar was beneath an out of business restaurant and the cracked sidewalks.

Half of the six grab tables while the rest of us were needed to carry the pitchers. We instantly broke out the drinking games to get our quick buzz to hopefully signify the beginning over a horrible headache the next morning. Laughter ensued as tipsy people tried to get out of buying their share of beer. We argued about rounds, bitched about professors, bullshitted about life.

Returning from one of my bathroom visits I ran into Jarred.

"Hey, ya drunk bastard!" I bellowed at him.

Grinning, he said, "Aye, but I ain't the only drunk"

I had to think about this one, "…Good point, come let us get a pitcher of the water down stuff and forget ourselves."

"Twist my arm a little harder Leif."

"Ah shit, you remembered my name, that more than what I can say."

"Jarred."

"That is right, ha, I will more than likely forget that two more times."

"No bother, the only reason I remember your name is that it is that I heard one of your patriots over there shout it out."

"Ah, so you wanted me to feel like a jackass eh Jarred."

"Yep."

"I can live with that, lets go."

Jarred and I proceeded to close the bar down; we jeered at women, taunted freshmen, and drank our bellies full. He proceeded to ask me about Chris. I was drunk so I let out the goods to him. I told him of all her amazing qualities and her little quirks like when she gets flustered and shakes her head about. When she is deep in thought and I just stare at her until she remembers and then she smiles with just the littlest of tongues sticking out. How everything seems okay when I am with her. It seemed as I told Jarred he could remember a girl just like her. I was getting carried away with the talk when a bouncer approached us telling us to finish them up and to move on. I slammed my beer and got up and fell down. Jarred just look at me with disappointment and then he got up and pulled me to his shoulder as we laughed our way out into the streets.

Never Fall in Love with a Vampire. It is a Pain in the Neck

Chapter 8

What a horrible morning or should I say afternoon when I woke. I found myself huddled in the corner of my room with one pant leg on and the rest of my clothes lying in various places of the apartment. I stood up only to land my ass back on the floor felling the headache; crawling seemed like the best alternative as I made my way to the bathroom. The tile of the floor was cold as I grabbed the vanity and pulled my body up. Looking in the mirror I let out a cry of pain. I washed my face and lapped up water with my tongue to wash away the morning after drink. After five minutes of loathing and ridiculing myself I left the bathroom and made my way to the living room. Everything seemed dusky in the afternoon sun as I sat down on the sofa. To sick to smoke I just stared at the ceiling. In retrospect, I remembered how well I felt when I give up the partying. How my body heals itself after only a few short weeks, better sleep, thinner face, thinner waistline for that fact, clear mind. Maybe I should stop the party for a while and return to that former self. Hours went by thinking of the consequences, causes, effects, and repercussions of my lifestyle. No clear answer came to my mind then again rarely does such answers, just move on with the lessons. With all my pandering, I did not notice the flashing red light next to my thinking. Finally after meeting my fate and feeling well enough for a smoke I noticed the blimp of the light. There was a message on my answering machine from Chris wanting to see me tonight.

I proceeded to clean up and went down to the school's pool for a sobering dip. After a brisk swim I proceeding to the library to do some studying for the next week. I fell asleep in the library; why do the libraries at universities have the most comforting chairs. I awoke with just a little bit of drool on the book, and placed it back up on the shelf and walked out the door. It was getting late and Chris would be expecting my call soon. Walking through the campus, I find an inner peace sometimes passing the buildings of which so much life and knowledge have existed and inspired over the years. The walkways that lead to every nook and cranny, through the quads of grass where the buildings just come up to the edge green as if they came from the earth themselves.

When I made it back to my apartment after taking some detours through the college of fine art and some little paths through the dorm buildings, I called Chris.

"What took you so long?"

"Sorry I fell asleep at the library."

"Again?"

Chris Crase

"Yep, I think they spike the water there and then sexually abuse people as they sleep."

"That is a pretty good idea."

"Yeah, but I tell you my ass is killing me."

"Ha, well I was thinking about going to a coffee shop tonight. I know of one with a open mike night and thought I could hear some of your poetry."

"You actually want to listen to me spurt forth some ridiculous prose?"

"Yea, and who knows I might do one too."

"Now that is something I would like to see. Why don't you come over and get me."

"I will be there in 20 minutes."

"See you then Chris."

I put the phone down and looked around the apartment. 20 minutes to clean up and to clean myself up. Not a problem. I went and grabbed ashtrays to dispose of them; soda cans, there must be hundreds of these suckers. Half way there, I picked up the dirty clothes that seem to hang from every where in the room. Maybe I will introduce a new type of wall decoration, and I will call it clothesline. After five minutes I was wiping off the coffee stained counters in the kitchen and throwing the dishes in the sink. I turned on a fan and opened windows to air out the infestation that brewed. I hopped into the shower and cleaned up in three minutes. I jumped out and proceeded to move to the bedroom. On my way there I see Chris sitting on the couch looking at one of my class books. Damn she beat me, I stood there caught because I still had two trash bags waiting to carry out.

"Hey," I said dripping away on the carpet.

"Looks like I caught you with your pants down."

"Good thing I left my towel on this time otherwise you would have caught a lot less. That really does not sound good does it maybe I should say you would see a lot more."

"That is something I would like to see."

"In your dreams Chris."

"Nah, In my dreams you have leather chaps on and a cowboy hat."

"Well, my chaps are at the cleaners."

"Darnn."

"Changing the subject, not that it wasn't interesting but I might start showing my not so manhood through this towel. Would you like a drink?"

"How about some tea."

"Sure." I went and grabbed two cups and put on some water.

"Now, if you will excuse me. I would like to put on some clothes."

Never Fall in Love with a Vampire. It is a Pain in the Neck

"Can I watch Leif?"

"That did it." I grabbed the front of my crotch and leapt into my room.

I could hear Chris laughing in the living room. As I disposed of my towel and proceeded with putting on my boxers and jeans. After a couple of minutes looking for some clean socks, I emerge to be greeted with my cup of tea in the kitchen.

"Thank you, how is it?"

"Not bad, I have had better but then again haven't we all had better."

"Are we still talking about the tea?"

"Perhaps."

I take a sip, "Oh, well yes I definitely have had better." producing a grin which was received by a punch to the shoulder.

"Thanks a lot."

"Oh, excuse me, you can dish it out but can't take it?"

"Oh believe me Leif, I can definitely take it." this time Chris making a grin.

I play dumb, "Is this have sexual innuendo in it."

"You are the one who made the tea." Chris following my lead.

"I knew I should have made Earl Grey."

Before Chris could say something I stole a kiss, which she reciprocated. After a good twenty seconds this time we pulled away and took our tea to the couch.

"So, what did you do today?" I asked Chris.

"Not much, just wandered about the city, looking for trinkets and various shops and stuff, ya know."

"Find anything good?"

"Oh, yes I found these clothes and had some wonderful bagels at this odd little shop that was a café too in a weird way. And how was your day?"

"Same'ol, same'ol life at the school. You do look nice though in your new old clothes. I was going to say something but I have the tendency to compliment the wrong thing on a women."

"How do you mean?"

"Well, if a girl, say, gets a haircut. I would mistakenly comment on her shoes as being new, or if she got a new top, I would say when did you get a haircut? I am not very attentive to those things even though I can notice a difference I just can pick up on it."

"So you are saying I go though all the trouble of sprucing up for you and you won't even know it."

"Are you trying to get me in trouble with my words."

"Yep."

Chris Crase

"Oh, well ya see, I would love to give you compliments like that and be right all the time it is just I cannot get past your smile and eyes to notice anything else." I hope that saved me.

"Nice recovery Leif, but I saw right through it."

"Did it work?"

"Yeah, for now. Anyhow shall we be going?"

"Okay, just let me find my books."

I rambled around my apartment looking for the various folders and notebooks that I have put writings in over the years. After about five minutes I had my pack full of poems, math problems, chemistry lab books, and whatever.

"Those are not all your poems are they?"

"Nah, usually I write in class when it gets boring so I use those notebooks where I should keep notes and stuff, I should organize them someday."

"Tell me about it look at my poem book."

Chris walks over to the kitchen counter and garbs into her purse and pulls out a small drafting book. "See all my poems are contained in this little book."

Surprised I say, "Chris I did not know you wrote poetry?"

"Well, sometimes at night I do not sleep very well and I get bored so I write."

"Excellent, let's go then."

Chapter 9

There was a couple of coffee shops down near the campus, and we went to one where I have never been before. It was beneath the street, probably a storage room for the store above it years ago. The shop was dimly lit with some jazz in the background. My eyes glanced over the dusty brick walls looking at pictures of student artwork. The shop was a little empty and we stole a table in one of the darkest corners below a huge painting. I commented to Chris about the painting which was one of the better ones there. She smiled and told me to sit as she was treating me to some coffee. She walked off as I did some more casing of the joint. One student was busy fumbling away on a laptop, some more are engaged with meaningless, that is meaningless to everyone that was not engaged in it themselves, conservation. One couple was on a date and then there was a group of college students that looked like they were here for the open mike night. One of the coffee shop employees was busy setting up a make shift stage. Under track lighting, the stage consisted of a stool and a microphone stand next to a bar counter. It was set in the opposite corner of the shop against the wall. Chris returned with a couple of drinks, mine a coffee loaded with cream and some sugar just the way I like it. She sat down and began to converse about the crowd. A couple of people had guitars but most had pieces of paper. Some were writing some stuff on napkins while their friends encourage them.

The first up on the stage was a couple from the large group. The girl strapped on a guitar while the guy proceeding to sing a quite good rendition of a popular song that I just cannot remember the name of. The crowd cheered as they continued for two more songs. One of their friends went up next as the two left and read from a napkin. Napkin poetry and art is somewhat underrated in my opinion, so many great ideas and inspired moments that Wordsworth himself would be proud of. Most of my moments come under a buzz of the beer and a flick of the cigarette as I scramble and harass the bartender for pens and napkins, while in coffee shops it is easier as all the utensils are readily available. Napkins and paper towels hover over notebooks as forethoughts, afterthoughts. One night I remember I talked with a deaf man for hours as napkins were our only means of communication. We talked love, hate, past, memories that made us smile. Napkin art: one of the last remaining proofs that we indeed are human.

After a hour the stage was abandoned as everyone lost their nerve. Chris motioned to me to get up there. Feeling like I was caught between

Chris Crase

something and something else I scrimmaged through my bag. I found one that I wrote a couple years back when I took a two week road trip. I made my way to the stage as all the eyes fell upon me, the person trying to salvage, what was up to then, a better than average open mike night. I went into acting mode as I tried to let the stares not bother me. I began to speak very upbeat in the mike.

"What city in the black earth do I approach?
Driving down the freeway in my girl, an old rusted car that is my soul
City that my eyes never seen what is your name?
Mobile, AL. Ahhh, but is it a city or the dragon, society?
A tunnel through I go purging the monster's throat emerging a phoenix.
This is no creature of death.
A beautiful night enhanced by the city's lights,
people's dreams, life, good or bad. It doesn't matter.
These humans too have aspirations in this dragon.
Are mine anymore important, do they care?
Bah! Quit questioning everything.
I only wish to learn. Learn?
I want it all.
How frustrating, knowing I will not even touch the tip of the iceberg.
Good, I'll just keep flying through the sky till dawn when I fall in a fiery streak
into the tide of failure.
Perhaps... but I will fly again
unless I stop believing I can.
Grow up they say. Why?
As a kid I believed in the impossible.
Nothing is...
My mind and soul will make it happen.
I am a god!
What will happen to me on this flight?
I do not know, do not care.
I just know life happens,
the greatest class to ever be taught by the teacher, me."

Either I was really bad or worse than that. I proceeded down the table sat at where Chris was. She just looked at me. I downed my now lukewarm coffee and put away my notebook.

"Maybe we should get out of here before I get lynched." I said.

Never Fall in Love with a Vampire. It is a Pain in the Neck

"What are you talking about, look around, you left everyone in a new thought. What more can you ask for. You want to shoot the stars? Don't you?"

"It is all I have"

The owner came over with a fresh cup of coffee and put in front of me.

"Excellent, that was great" he said.

"Well thank you, I was just going for 'well at least I spoke clearly.'"

"Nah, man, that was killer."

I looked around and was greeted by some people nodding in approval the rest went on with their conversation. The owner returned to the counter to wait on some girls.

"You see Leif, it was really good."

"Well, now it is your turn."

"I don't think so."

"Come on I did it."

"I do guess I owe you now huh."

"Yep, and calling in you debt."

"Give me a second." Chris starts to flick through her book.

I try to steal a glance at her writing only to catch some sketches. Meanwhile the open mike night continues with yet another poet. Chris quickly found a poem that she felt was adequate. However, more and more amateur poets began to sweep out of the walls as the stage became littered with napkins, and notebook paper. I spotted an artist in one of the corners left drawing away at some of the people on stage. Chris and began to inquire about each others past relationships. Why does it seem that we as a society muddling through this life feel the need to measure ourselves against past boyfriends and girlfriends? And then somehow we are perturbed that this person has been in other relationships. What is this jealousy? Ah, but remember you have done the same. Remember we are all guilty of this and a true test of all things is can we live with our pasts as well as learn along the way. As the conversation continued, poet after singer made their way up on the stage until the owner came up and said it was time to go. We looked around realizing that we had left the crowd some time ago as we were the last people in here except for the owner mopping the floor.

"Oh man, I did not get to hear your poem."

"I am somewhat relieved I am not very good at public speaking."

"Wait… you do not get out that easy." as I turn to the owner "She would like to read her poem but had the stage frights. Can she get up there now and do it before we check out."

"Why not, go on get up there." as the owner took my drift and egged her on.

Chris Crase

Chris smiles as she get up "You are gonna pay for this."

"I bet, don't you need your book?

"Nope I am gonna improvise."

Chris made her way up to the stage. The owner took a place next to me with his forearm on the mop. She breathed into the mike looking right at me.

"I lie awake some nights
wondering where he is
if he even exists at all
It starts to rain as I look out
into the and past the raindrops
on the windows
I know what he looks like
I know what he thinks
I know, I know what he feels
I know what I want
But why can't I find him
Maybe he does not exist
Or maybe I found something else
Something unexpected and yet not
Maybe I knew what I wanted more than what was in my dreams
Perhaps my thoughts only prevented me from finding him
and maybe he is sitting right in front of me"

The owner nudged me with a grin.

"Sounds to me you have some stuff to talk about. I have pretty much a full pot of coffee still. I will bring it out and you two take your time."

All right now I am pretty nervous, Chris had got me off guard. The only thing I could say when she sat down was, "Well, your poem was obviously better than mine because I only got a cup of coffee while the owner is getting you an entire pot."

"I guess that was pretty good for winging it" She smiled as she filled up her cup.

"What is happening to us? I mean are we, you know uh, starting to really like each other? Or is this just a crush or..."

Chris grabs my hand, "Who knows, why are ya worried? I thought nothing got to you."

"Relationships have been a sore spot on my past. It seems that when I find myself interested or visa versa I tend to run. Maybe not running like ditching town or breaking but then again that is not out of the question. I could just change my personality such that you cannot stand me any more."

"Are you scared of relationships?"

"I do not believe so, I think I am capable of such things but I think more that with past relationships they haven't been right as far as where I want to go with it. It is either can I change her to something or can she change me into something. I would much rather be in a mutual changing relationship that does not trivialize important things to us and overdue the trivial things." Grinning in thought, "Of course the key is finding out what are the trivial and not trivial isn't it. Most of the time I won't even bother with that."

"Well then how about just hanging until we figure it out or if that doesn't happen then we can keep hanging knowing we cannot figure it out."

"Ya see, there you go again making sense of it all." Smiling at her.

"Let's get out of here."

We picked up are things and walked back to my pad. I talked to her about my classes: which one I enjoyed, which ones I hate, the class mates, the professors. At my place, I figured it would be better just to end the night and my uneasiness. I told her that I had a pretty busy schedule but Wednesday I can get away for a few hours. I also told her that I was not making this up because of what transpire and if I could get away earlier than that I would. Christine appreciated that, I could tell she was feeling that I was getting spooked. I stood by her car as she drove off and then proceeded to go in my apartment to get some sleep for the next couple of days. Needless to say I did not sleep very well.

On the way home, Christine stopped off at a blood bank in Beverly Hills to quench her appetite. Contrary to belief, vampires do not need to feed nightly. Once a week is pretty much all right to keep them quite sufficient. Christine arrived back at home; she tossed her purse down and made her way to the living room. She smiled thinking about the night as she went into the bathroom to wash up. Emerging in her robe she was met by a figure in her bedroom.

"Hello, Christine"

"Jarred, is that you."

"How have things been?"

"What are you doing here? Last I heard you were in Seattle."

"I came in a couple of months ago, Seattle was a bit too wet for me."

"So what have you been up too."

"I should ask you the very same question."

"What do you mean by that" Christine starts to get a little on edge and goes to retrieve a cigarette.

Chris Crase

"This Leif character, I have been watching you too he has fallen for you pretty bad."

"I hadn't notice we have been just having fun."

"Don't play coy with me Christine."

"I don't know what you are getting at."

"Listen we both know the rules, you can't go out falling for these humans it just leads to trouble every time that is why we have to follow guidelines."

"You have been watching us haven't you."

"Yes."

"Great now you are my big brother or some father figure."

"I am only looking out for you and all of us."

"I can take care of myself."

"Then start by taking care of Leif."

"I cannot do that."

"I was going to do it for you on numerous occasions but I figured if I did you would not have talked to me for the next some odd hundred years like what happened with that other guy in the old land."

"Yea, well with Leif it is different."

"I do not care if it is different, I do not want to get the council involved in this."

"You don't have too."

"That depends on you Christine."

"Go to hell."

"Listen, when are you seeing him next."

"Wednesday."

"Finish him then okay then nothing more will become of this."

"I don't know if I can."

"Christine, either do it Wednesday or I will step in. I would rather have you not talk to me for a few centuries than to have to bring in the council. You know how much they hate coming to the states."

"Fine, goodnight Jarred."

"Night."

Christine sat down with another cigarette and watch the city lights, a tear began to form in her eye, Christine had not cried since she was first reborn. Damn her life.

The next couple of nights, Christine could not tolerate. She would awake before dusk and lay around thinking out what to do. She wanted to tell Leif everything and then she didn't. Christine rationalized everything to death and then when that did not work she went for emotional and after that the gut instinct. Nothing could satisfy her questions, duty. She wanted forgiveness for her sins of life; she knew though there is no absolution like in the fairytales. The only way she made herself feel better was taking out a couple of gents at the nightclubs around the town. The first night was a middle aged man who made it a habit of hitting on younger women. The second night was a guy about twenty-eight who was married and could not stay faithful. The third night was an out of town business man who was also married. Christine was in a very vengeful mood. Somehow axing, the rotten trees made her feel a smaller bit of guilt of what she had to do or just hid it by repeatable guilt. The next day she did not sleep; she lay awake during the day hearing her next door neighbors rumble about with groceries and kids.

The night came quickly and the phone rang. She rolled over herbed and picked up the receiver.

"Hello?"

"Hey, Chris it is Leif."

"Hi."

"You sound a little troubled, anything bothering you?"

"Nah, I was just taking a quick nap and I am still kinda of drowsy."

"Oh, I did not mean to wake you."

"That is okay, I am in the mood for a drink, actually for a lot of drinks."

"That is why I like you so much, meet me at the jazz club by my place."

"All right."

"Bye."

Christine put down the phone and got up and proceeded to shower. She figured that getting me drunk would make it less painful on me. She did not want to waste time on getting ready so she put on a T-shirt and jeans and left.

I arrived at the bar, too bad there is no live music tonight but the owner still had an excellent collection of albums he and his father collected. The bar was very dark, even more so than most bars. The mood was of the Big Easy as the music resonated of the old wood walls covered in vintage photographs, not those cheesy reproductions we see in all family grills. The air was moist with smoke from cigars, cigs, joints and clung to your eyes and clothes. The tables were old worn wood found in garage sales of a time since gone. The wood seemed to have soaked up all the bourbon that was ever filled in that bar and returned the smell twice fold with its own flavor included.

I sat down and signaled hello to the bartender. He quickly poured me a pint and danced his way over to me. The album playing was one of his favorites. I lit up a smoke and began to drink. Chris arrived a few moments later and pulled up the stool against me. My back was turned so I did not

Chris Crase

see her. She tapped me on my shoulder a moved to the other side of myself. I looked back to see no one. Knowing that she got me, I turned the other way very slowly with a little grin. She was looking at me with big bright innocent eyes and her lips curled up in a smirk. My only response to that was to throw her into a headlock and give her a noggie. She pushed me away with a little disgust look on her face at she swiveled her hips toward the bar ignoring me.

"Okay." I got up and pushed my shoulders forward and rolling my neck, "Enough play time now you must be destroyed."

Chris raised an eyebrow, looked at me and then proceeded to punch me in the belly. I fell to one knee.

"Okay, so I cannot destroy you but can I get you a beer?" I said with a smile.

"Good boy." she responded.

"You seem to be in a frisky mood tonight."

"Nah, just horny."

"All right I am gonna get some." looking at the bartender.

"Oh, gawd." Chris threw her hand to her eyes in embarrassment.

I sat back down and the bartender delivered a beer with a naughty grin. I lit Chris' cigarette as well as one for myself.

"How were classes?"

"Horrible, ah the pain and misery."

"What happen?"

"I got an A on one test and then I got another A, then another."

"Oh, poor thing"

"So how are you?"

"Pretty good, my job kept me busy this week and I almost was not able to meet you here tonight."

"Really, well I am glad you made it."

"Yeah, I managed to finish up today I am in the mood to drink now."

"Good, me too. First come and dance with my sweet."

"Of course, Don Juan."

The bar was pretty dead so we were able to clear away some of the tables enough to move. Another, older black couple joined in and showed us some grooves. We danced and drank for a good hour then tired we retreated to the bar again to just drink. We got started on the philosophies of a topic, as much bar talk goes to the drunks.

"Chris, tell me something," As I was entertaining a thought, "Where do you see man going in this world?"

"Man for the most part will die off as women will take over the world and I shall be their queen."

Never Fall in Love with a Vampire. It is a Pain in the Neck

"Alright, easy enough let me rephrase that there question. Where do you think the human race will end up?"

"All in all I think we are screwed. If you look at this place we have created, America in general, land of the free and home of the brave right. Well it would seemed to me by the events unfolding is that we are only concerned about freedom to the extent of profit for ourselves, to trade to keep cost down with the third world countries and to increase our wealth. We rape the world with less courtesy than a man has toward a woman all in the name of consumption at a low price. Man as you put it only seems interested in doing better like we are taught which means get what you can get. The only time we think about our consequences is when the resource has died and then because we are human we can rise above and develop something better or we see the effect of the cause through our blinded eyes and change but more or less we change only when it is necessitated. But in the course of it all the greed is the driving influence in humanity. This is what drives our so called freedom and rights and our work ethic and our being. With this attitude we are pretty much screwed as I said."

"Did you suck the thoughts out from my head or what? Are you an alien with some sort of brain wave capability? I agree with you on most points in your statement but alas I think I fall victim to idealism. Somehow I believe we will struggle through it, painful at times yes and the lesson will be learned but the struggle is important. More important than the human itself is the struggle to overcome our ignorance, the struggle to overcome our character flaw, the struggle over arrogance. Yes, Chris the lessons shall be learned along the way and hopefully we will not kill ourselves retaking the course over and over but perhaps one time we can pass. In our time we will see the unfortunate misgivings of ourselves, whether it be not aiding ourselves over national pride or conflict. Death, war will happen, famine, disease, life will happen and the key is to learn, adapt, struggle forth not to let all of it happen till one day the struggle pays off and it does not happen. The struggle for human dignity."

"Can we though considering ourselves and our nature?"

"That is why I am the idealistic fool, I think we can."

"You do know that the idealists are usually shot first."

"Yes but we usually go out in a way that a movie will be made about us after fifty years or so. But you are right we come to terms with ourselves at this point in our development so the struggle right now is less important. It is still there though and it will gain in time. It is too bad that we create out of necessity and not from common sense."

Chris Crase

"Some would say you could break your heart with all that hope for humanity. Ya know trying to find it somewhere in this world only to be let down each and every time."

"Well at least I can say I have a heart when the game is done. Besides there are few things have seen that keeps it going, not much but some. But enough of this drunken talk."

Putting down another beer I can feel the spirits start to take control. And I that note I went to the bathroom.

Christine sat there and lit a cigarette, thinking to herself. She knew why she had fallen for this person. He just said it, idealism. Still after all these years Christine has not been able to rid herself of the memory of humanity. That was the very reason she fell for Jacob. Fading away from the bar in the smoke, Christine remembers Jacob from previous times and worlds. A world wrought in change. Change for the lesser people in the world. A time when the world was collapsing under the ideas of the old and reborn in a promise of equality. And then there was Jacob a happen chance peddler who was educated on the streets and born again under the extreme prejudices of old and new. Christine found him one night after he tried to rob her room. She was renting out in the old world while casually mixing with the upper elite. Taking her pleasures at night with the folks she returned in the middle of the night to find Jacob wearing her necklaces and stuffing rings into his pocket. Both taken back by the awkwardness of the situation Jacob tried to rush her only to trip over her stool and fall onto his face putting a cut into his forehead. The sudden rush caused Christine to gasp from the shock and fall into her love seat. She managed however to see the clumsy Jacob hurt his pride more than anything else. He looked up at her as the blood slowly came from his head. The bewildered look but Christine over the edge and she broke into a tearful laugh.

Jacob feeling his own humility began to laugh as well. He stood up and started to take off the woman's garments and place then back on the table. A spot of blood fell on her silk scarf that laid next to the return belongings. Jacob at once apologized for the mess. Christine regained herself and took him aside to care for the wound with her scarf. She told him not to worry about the scarf as she took it from the mistress' party on another occasion. They both had a good laugh at that.

The next night Jacob was waiting for Christine as she returned from a gala. Again she was shocked but they spent the rest of the night talking away their lives. Christine and Jacob grew fond of one another and their midnight interludes. Most of the nights were spent around wine and cheese as Christine taught Jacob how to read and write while Jacob filled in the frustration of the life as a street rat. Weeks turned into a year and half and

Never Fall in Love with a Vampire. It is a Pain in the Neck

Jacob had been spending most of his night in a cell at that point for public speaking. Christine would meet him sometimes at the cell and they would continue their affair with bars separating them.

Unbeknownst to Christine was the careful watch of Jarred. He was in town as well and stayed apart from Christine as she preferred it such. Jarred however under the guise of shadows and a crush led him to the discovery of Jacob. And so it was that one night while Jacob was behind chains once again, Jarred paid him a visit. Jacob was hoping that Christine would soon show and was busy scribbling down a poem for her arrival when he was overcome by Jarred. Christine all but arrived when Jarred was cleaning up his mark to reveal a suicide. Jarred thought befitting after reading the poem. A romantic suicide fit so well for the street rat.

Christine returns back in time to the present as the music changed over and once got in thought over Leif. No wonder she thought. Still human after all these years she thought to herself. One thing I have not been able to rid myself of is that I am a sucker for the fool hearted. Perhaps one day but I cannot go through that pain again. No it is better this way. I may fall for the idiot savant, but I am what I am there is no changing that. She turned back to the bar and ordered more drinks waiting for Jacob, um Leif to comeback from the jail.

When I returned from the bathroom, Chris had greeted me with another beer.

"Did I ever tell you I love you?"

Chris looked at me kinda cheesy and said "No".

"Not you wench!! I was talking to the beer." Smirking at the beer not giving her an inch.

"All right smart ass, let's get it on." Smirking back.

"No way! you already kicked my butt earlier. I prefer getting in little cheap shots instead for the rest of the night."

"I guess I can put up with that."

I sat back down on the barstool and got out a smoke. Lighting it up, I mumbled very softly, "I do by the way."

Chris obviously heard me, but ignored it and played dumb stating "What, you say something?"

"Would you like a smoke, I noticed you were out."

"Yeah, thank you."

"Chris, do you play pool?"

"I have been know to dabble in a game or two."

"Would you like to play?"

"Why not."

Chris Crase

Dabble my ass, Chris proceed to beat me three out of four times. The only reason I won one game is that I made her screw up a shot on the eight ball by referring to a piece of her anatomy that stuck out when she was shooting. I know it was bad taste but geeze I could not lose them all. We went and danced some more all the while drinking. When the placed finally closed, I was in no condition to even walk home so I figured that Chris was pretty drunk too.

"Listen I do not want you driving home so you can crash at my place."

"Oh, like I have not heard that line before." Chris smirking.

"Hey all I am saying is that there is one be and one couch you choose one and I will take the other."

"Okay, you are probably right any way."

"Of course I am right. I have good judgment about these things as I proceeded to trip over a line painted on the road.

When we got back to my place, I proceeded to get a glass of water for Chris and myself. She excused herself to the bathroom. I threw on some tunes and got a blanket for the couch sleeper. I lit up a smoke as I sat down to drink some more water. Chris emerged in one of my T-shirts. I was so caught off guard that I dropped my smoke and put a nice burn hole on the chair. Flustered, I shot up retrieving the smoke and extinguishing it, cursing myself.

"Why Leif, you look a little shocked?"

"Oh that, no that always happens when I sit in that chair" Scratching my head and pondering the chair. "I mean it had nothing to do with the fact you are standing in my living room with just a T-shirt and I hope your scibbies."

"Yes, my underwear is still on, geeze Leif it is like you have never been around a girl before."

"Well, I mean uh well, I have to brush my teeth excuse me."

I went into the bathroom and just stared at my reflection. I was thinking that this was heaven and hell. Maybe I am religious. I would love to be with her but at the same time I like her so much that I do not want to blow this. Brushing the canines, I thought that maybe I will just tell her that "Hey you can crash with me but I am very tired and I do have class tomorrow." I washed my face and put on some more deodorant and left. I walked out to see the light turned out and my reading light on in my room. I walked in to see Chris under the covers.

"This bed is very uncomfortable."

"But it was cheap, that is all that matters. Listen Chris I don't know what you are expecting but I am gonna lay it out for you. I like you actually like you a lot but I do not want to mess this up so I mean I can sleep here with you but I do not want it to get carried away."

Never Fall in Love with a Vampire. It is a Pain in the Neck

"Okay, I do not want to make this uncomfortable, or do I?" grinning.

"Unforgiving is more like it. The thing is that we had had a lot to drink and I do not know maybe I am cheesy or something but I do not think it is right being drunk and all is a good idea."

"Are you afraid that I will be disappointed?" still grinning.

"Well, that would probably happen whether or not I am drunk, actually it might be a good idea cause then I could use that as an excuse." Smirking.

"Sounds like you are not very confident in your libido."

"Okay well I just do not us to wake up tomorrow with huge hangovers and then having this hang over our heads. I have done that too many times and I haven't had a good experience at anytime with it."

"I know what you are saying though I haven't had a good experience either, always not a mistake but rather an 'Ah shit I did it again'. But haven't you always said I was different?"

"Yeah, I have said that haven't I?"

"So who is to say tomorrow will be an 'Ah, shit?"

"You have got me there, as I always say lets throw caution against the wind."

"Well, then come to bed."

The next two hours, was something out of a miracle. Not even a miracle could describe the emotions that were found and conceded to more unfounded emotion. As we as one explored the avenues of our relationship, likeness could only be found in the universe of a beautiful dancing symphony of madness, violence, death, rebirth, fire, redemption. We laid there as the crescent moon shined unto our bodies. Chris upon my bare chest, bare chested as the covers only needed to keep the floor warmth. Nothing was said as the moonlight cooled our bodies, I wanted that moment frozen in time and begged the moon to do so. I wanted to die with this being my last memory. And with that I closed my eyes.

Christine did not sleep; she just laid there trying to think of a way to get out of this. Rationalizing the consequences of every possible action she could take. It always came down to that if she did not go through with it the council would end up having someone else do it and it would not be kind hearted. She would be the message the warning. It was approaching dawn and Christine had to make a quick retreat. Leif was completely passed out. She leaned over him and kissed him and then proceeded to bear her fangs upon his neck. She tried to do it as softly as possible but once the rich blood hit her lips she proceed to indulge herself. Christine started to cry as she tried to control her urge. When she finished she rushed to the bathroom and threw up. Wiping away the blood from her chin, she got dressed and left the apartment. She figured since she did not hide her handy work the cops would just suspect one of the many occults in L.A. that practice vampirism.

When she got back to her place, she went into her room as day broke and just laid in her bed with the darkness upon her. Her thoughts keep her company until night came again.

Chapter 10

The next week Christine spent most of her nights just wandering the streets. She made her way down to the beach sometimes and walked along the surf. Sometimes she would gently float across the coves to the other side. One night Christine went back to the piano bar on the hunt. She was at the bar just drinking away her sorrows wondering why the men were avoiding her. The bartender came up to her and began to converse with her. They were carrying on for a few minutes when Christine asked a question.

"Do I have ugly zit on my face that just exploding or something? Cause usually I can attract half the men in here."

"No Miss but the reason I think that they are avoiding you is because you are carrying around a heavy heart."

"Really, I did not think I showed."

"Most people with a broken heart are able to have men or women hit on them in a bar to try to get over it. But you don't want to get over him and it shows, he must have been something special."

"He was incredible. It shows that bad huh?"

"Lady I have been bar tending for twenty years and you are the second person I have ever come across that when they enter a bar the opposite sex just looks up and turns away cause they know they will never offer you any thing better than what you had."

"Who was the other?"

"My bother in law when my sister passed away."

"Oh I am sorry."

"Don't be he had a life that few will ever have. If you don't mind me asking what happened to you."

"He made me feel alive, again. In a word of the mouth he would stimulate the soul and make me see again what was lost to years of living. Then my family pushed him away cause he was different."

"Your family must be some hard asses. Here let me get you another drink."

Christine lit up a cigarette and thought, "He has know idea how tough they are."

Glancing up at the piano player, Christine became lost in thought of Leif. She looked around at the people in the bar. All of these humans enjoying themselves, some with cares others with none. All of them alive. How lucky they are to be able to wake up in the morning and see the sun, feel its heat. Maybe they wake up next to a love one maybe not; and though they only live a few short years, they are alive. Alive to make mistakes,

Chris Crase

make accomplishments, to dwindle, to grow, whatever their lot they had the choice. Whereas most of these people will go into their weekly routine on Monday unknowingly living. Are they content? Who knows. I would give up eternity if she could live they next day with him again.

"So tell me about him." The bartender returns with a drink.

"Well lets see..." Christine gets a smile on her face, "His was an adventurous soul who like a kid saw the world for the first time, every time, he never tried to limit himself and did what he could to do the best in life. He often spoke of the sins of living and that there was no absolution to such sins. All that could be done is just living."

"What do you mean by or should I say him by the sins of living?"

"Hmmm, I would imagine he would say something like, 'ya know the sins of living,' he would make you think about and wait for an answer. I think for him it would be something like loving is a sin, caring is a sin, not helping, helping day in day out doing the best to make it through life only to get out dead and then when on your last seconds of life not even realizing the life. Ya know 'sins'."

"He sounds to much like my older brother." The bartender grinning at a memory.

"Then you know."

"Believe me Miss,"

"Call me Christine, please."

"Okay, Christine believe me my sis was something special, she was always tramping over the world seeing things here and there. Sometimes it would have been weeks or a year before we heard from her. She was amazing like that and then one day she came into town with this hubby. I liked the guy right away, nothing hiding in his face just there. Always willing to lend a hand, always looking for something. Ah, sometimes I wish he was still around."

"He passed away?"

"Nah, not that I know of. They had a kid you see and after the funeral and a few months of lulling around he took off with the kid. None of the family was happy with this, even my folks and other bro took to the police. They still haven't found him it has been what 5 years. I will let ya in a secret though. I ain't pissed at him I knew his nature and this is what my sis would have wanted." He reaches under the bar, "Here is a postcard I got from him a month ago from Japan. He writes to me from time to time to let me know how it is going."

Looking over the postcard, Christine says, "I think Leif and your Brother would get along marvelously."

"Yeah, they probably would," looking down the bar, "It looks like I am needed, nice talking with ya Christine and keep your chin up if he is the guy you say he is he won't let your family get in the way."

"I hope you are right."

Christine sat around the bar in her new muse. Knowing that she showed a heavy heart she looked out at the people of the bar. Wanting their thoughts on her to hear their condolences. She had a few more drinks and smokes as the night carried on, after awhile she grew tired and retreated back into the city of angels.

Chapter 11

The next night Christine found herself at the beach again. Just drifting along with her sandals in one hand and a cigarette in the other. There was a late night bon fire and volleyball party going on. She slipped in for a few drinks. She could not get in the mood for fun and games so she split. Walking further down the beach, she approached some familiar lights. She could not quite place them so intrigued she walked toward them. It was that bar and grill that Leif took her too. Looking rather dead cause of the party up the way, she decided to go in and have a drink. She walked up to the bartender and had a glass of wine.

"I remember you." Charlie said to Christine.

"You do?" Christine lighting a cigarette.

"Yeah, you were that one girl that Leif fell head over heels."

"Oh he told you that."

"Sure did, Leif doesn't let on but me and him go back a few." winking at Christine. "Yep he was quite broken up about losing you."

"How do you mean?"

"He has been in here almost every night this past week, talking and drinking, talking and drinking."

"This past week?"

"Yeah, in fact he is here tonight with all his school buddies over there."

"He stepped out for a second, though to grab some smokes, ya see my machine isa broke. But he should be back pretty soon. Oh looks like thirsty people over there are a getting angry. Nice seeing ya."

Christine went to the bathroom. How could he be alive still? I thought I had sucked almost everything I could from his body. It is impossible, Charlie must be crazy, unless I did not finish him. That would mean he is one of us now. Oh gawd, I have really done it now when the council hears about this. Then again they have made exceptions to the conversion process before. Maybe. I wonder if Leif knows yet. It does take awhile some times. Morgan told me he did not know for two months. The sun bothered him a little and he was thirsty for blood but until he took his first victim he was still pretty much human. I wonder if Leif is back. Why hasn't he called?

Christine emerged from the bathroom to see me waiting for her at the bar.

"Hey Leif, how are you?"

"I am doing well I guess."

"That is good to hear."

Never Fall in Love with a Vampire. It is a Pain in the Neck

"Are you mad at me?"

"Me, no! Why would you think that?"

"Well when I woke that morning there was no you, no note, no nothing so I thought I pissed you off or something."

Thinking quickly Christine responds "I just needed some time to work things out but why did you not call me?"

"I did but your answering machine has been turned off and I could never get you."

"Oh, well… uh… what now?"

"Well if you are not mad at me then you want a drink?"

"Yes." Christine jumps on the stool next to me.

"So what have you been up to?"

"Nothing really just reading and walking the streets. What have you been up to?"

"Well, I have been busy trying to not think about you because of the forth said so I have been at the beach during the day. I went to Frisco last weekend with some of the guys sitting over there."

"Fun in the sun eh?"

"Yea h, I got a pretty good tan eh?"

"The sun doesn't bother you?"

"Nah, even though I am pretty fair skin I do not sunburn much."

"Really?"

"Yeah, me and the sun god get along pretty well, hey Charlie can we get some drinks."

Christine is pretty confused now. She glances at my neck to see her puncture wounds. None were found.

"So were you pretty hung over that morning?"

"Was I ever! Whoa, I spent the whole day in a bath just cleaning my body of that alcohol."

"Yea, I felt pretty bad too."

"Funny? I have noticed that alcohol doesn't affect you that much."

"Oh believe me it does, I can just hide it pretty well."

"You will have to teach me that trick."

"I will try, say you want to go for a walk on the beach?"

"Let's go."

We strolled under the diamond dusted sky. Unfortunately the city lights only brought the brightest of stars and there friends the planets. I told Christine of the stars in the mountains away from the city. Stars so many that would swear it was snowing and how they appear to be almost in reach. She just grinned as I carried on with the moon just dying over the ocean. I pointed out Orion.

Chris Crase

"Orion or Osiris they were both named after the same constellation: one the hunter the other the protector of the dead. It is just incredible to think that thousand of years ago our ancestors monitored these great explosions in the sky and then gave them names. As if they were our friends or lovers like the seven sisters."

"Yes they are quite amazing."

"Amazing?!, up there I mean that is it. That star over there could be just like ours and just like us there could be two people walking on that stars satellites wondering if they are alone. They could have the same hopes, same dreams, same problems. Or maybe they have it perfect whatever that is."

"Actually Leif, I think that is a planet."

"Huh?"

"Well yeah look at it. It does not twinkle like the rest."

"Hey, you are right."

"Of course I am."

"All right smart ass."

"Smart ass?!, You just do not like being one upped."

"Very true, it is not that I don't like it. That is awesome; I just do not like being caught off guard."

"That is something I do feel about you."

"Anyway, do you think the Mayans and the other ancients felt that awe that inspiration that wonderment at least I know I get when I gaze into heaven?"

"I don't know."

"Honest answer, I would like to think that they did though. I makes me think it is all worth it in some way."

"I would like to think that too."

We sat down on the beach for a while discussing the stars and the moon some more. I told Chris about the time when I was a kid and tried to build a kite out of every little piece of scrap I could find and tried to fly to the moon.

The kite was perfect in designed. I accounted for my small kid like body to be held like an X, I realized that it had to be light so I worked feverishly on the frame, making it from the lightest wood I could find in the woods. Every joint in the contraption was mold by my knife to fit precisely with each other. With the frame done all that was needed was the rope to hold me and the sail. I never thought much about controlling the damn thing as that doesn't concern the mind of a kid. The rope I took from my father's farm. The sail was a little most perplexing a task. Wool was too heavy as were most clothes at the time. The answer at the time was dried pig skin, so

Never Fall in Love with a Vampire. It is a Pain in the Neck

at the coming of the night I would tell my folks I was spending the night in the forest across the brook. When night came I ran off to the slaughter house on the other side of the village and scavenged all the skin I could get a hold off. It took another week to dry it and stitch it to a perfect sail. The morning after I finished the kite I was too exhausted to move so I slept in and figured on the next day being the one I shot for the moon. How jealous would all the people in the village be when they found out I went to the moon. I laid in my bed with a mischievous grin as I could not wait the glory.

The nest morning, I stood on the cliffs above my small town and strap into my flyer and waited to be swept up into the air and to the moon. A breeze came up and hit me. I thought it was gonna work as I felt my feet leave the ground. I screamed with joy until I realized I was being flung back. Fighting the once wanting breeze now I did my best to stay on the ground. However I was more busy keeping my balance that soon I was flung in the air, I was flying not very well mind you the wind did not want my burden so as soon as it lifted me it dumped me. I hit the ground a suffered a concussion and a few bruises. My father was pissed at my stupidity and cursed me as mom cared for my wounds. I was grounded for a week and put to work in the fields. Later that week my dad threw out his shoulder when he was trying to impress his buddies in the woods throwing axes. I walked into the kitchen that dusk after making modifications to my kite for a second test flight to see mom nursing him and cursing him. He looked at me and we both started to laugh. That weekend we out to the field to sail some kites.

Chris Crase

Chapter 12

Chris and I sat on the beach for a while longer listening to the surf as it began to encroach upon us. We got up and started to walk down the streets around the beach. The town was beginning to falter as the people slowly dispersed back to their homes. Only a few moving shadows bumped into ours as we walked down the street. We approached a street corner with the lamp out and was next to a desolate alley which seemed to cast its own darkness into the street. I noticed a figure standing next to the post of the light. His cigarette gave away his position. As we approached I recognized that is was Jarred.

"Hey, you wie Bastard!" shouted to him.

Extinguishing his cigarette he paid no attention to me. I felt Chris' grip tighten in my hand.

"What are you doing?" Jarred spoke to Chris with a stern voice.

"You two know each other?" I queried.

Still ignoring me, "Well Christine?"

"Leave me alone Jarred we will talk later."

"No, we are gonna talk now."

"Hey wait a minute, Jarred cool down you have drank too much tonight." I interjected.

"Shut up, you piece of human filth."

"All right Jarred we are gonna keep walking go and calm down." Feeling uncomfortable I tried to make amends.

"I said shut up!"

Chris spoke, "Jarred leave him alone this is between us."

"I told you to take care of him."

"And I thought I did." Chris exclaimed.

"You are leading yourself on with that dead heart of yours."

Totally confused I tried to get a word in "Hey Jarred."

At that point Jarred turned and faced me with red eyes. He opened his mouth to bare his truth. Before I could step back he already lunged onto my neck. He threw me into the alley as his teeth sunk deep into my neck. Jammed into the wall I felt my blood leaving me as my body began to go limp. I lost conscience. Jarred withdrew from his feast and threw my body to the ground. Wiping his face, he turned to Christine.

"There it is done."

Christine shocked at the display. "Why did you have to do that? I said I was gonna take care of him!"

"You told me that you were going to do that before."

Never Fall in Love with a Vampire. It is a Pain in the Neck

"And I did!"

"What do you mean?"

"I bit him, I really did, I thought I killed him and then I ran into him tonight."

"Jesus! You turned him? That could be more trouble."

"At first I thought I did but he hasn't gone through any of the transformation."

"What are you talking about, you are lying."

"No I swear I am not!"

"She is not lying." I stood up to face the two.

Jarred looked at me in disbelief, as did Chris. I brushed off the dirt from the alley as I began to slowly approach the two.

"So you two are vampires? I have heard about you guys just never bumped into one, let alone two." My eyes start to turn yellow as my anger is beginning to show.

Jarred spoke angrily "What is going on here?"

"You see Jarred, you can suck my blood but it replenishes you cannot turn me though because I already have been blessed or cursed however you want to look at it with an equally powerful disease."

"Stop this foolish talk!"

"I concur."

I rushed Jarred and grabbed him with both of my hands, as Chris stood frozen under the lamppost. I threw him to the ground in to alley as I walked toward him with conviction. My body began to turn to the wolf inside of me. Jarred looking right at me with fear of centuries past multiplied a hundred fold. He began to crawl backwards as I flung my claws and teeth onto him. Trying to resist I tossed his lanky body into the wall. Again he tried to retreat but I grabbed his ankle and pulled him under my jaws. An anguished scream came from his redden lips as my beast overcame my thought. Preying upon him I beared my teeth and swatted his battered face with my front paw. I could not let up on him; I would not let up on him as all my strength was gone and only the focused pain of the past enraged me. I tore the flesh from his body. Never letting him up, I pushed him, pushed him further into the alley. I have chosen the path. Jarred tried to scramble up a wall but my power drove him into the corner of trash. A crate broke his fall that is what I can remember too. My mind became blurred; jumping on him, I grabbed a makeshift stake from the broken box. Grasping with both paws, I arched my back holding his death in the stake high above. I looked into his weakened eyes and proceeded to drive my hatred into his chest as I howled with disgusted victory. Silence ensued as I made my way out of they alley to the frightened vampire. She looked at me with a different fear than what was in Jarred. Still disfigured, I paused in front of her beaming my yellow eyes into her scared soul. I heard a car coming down the street in the distances and was off. Across the street and into another alley and into the night.

Never Fall in Love with a Vampire. It is a Pain in the Neck

Chapter 13

I ran and ran through the streets and parks to the hills never once noticed. I ran until I was away from everything. Out of breath, I collapsed on the ground as the night behind the stars beat down its soothing silence. As I laid out upon a knoll I began to calm back to my normal self. Normal self? I am a man but yet a wolf intertwined. I was here in the woods in torn clothes, disgusted soul, and broken heart. Why in all the world I had to pick a vampire. Idiot, stupid fool. Maybe it is puppy love. No. The pack is not gonna like this. I fumbled around to see if my smokes remained intact. They were so I lit one up and started to make my way back to the town. It was a nice night.

On the other side of the city the play continues. Christine ran into her apartment just as dawn was breaking. She huddled in her dark room trying to gather some sense out of the night. Okay Jarred my long time friend killed my boyfriend whom I supposedly killed a couple a days ago. Jarred is now dead because my boyfriend turned out to be a werewolf. Now that Jarred is dead more will come to investigate his death by the council's will. Okay my boyfriend is a werewolf. How in the hell am I gonna tell the council that. Jarred is dead, and my boyfriend is a werewolf. Werewolf… What the hell is a werewolf anyway, I have seen them in movies they look rather ugly and poorly designed by the special effect artists. How the hell can they be real? What a ridiculous idea to have a werewolf in the same story as a vampire. Maybe Morgan will come and he will set things right, he has always helped me out. Then again my boyfriend is a werewolf.

I got back to my apartment and took a shower. I emerge in my living room in my towel and steam pouring off me. I laid down on the couch to some jazz and a cigarette. My girl is a vampire. No wonder she was never around during the day. I wonder if she is pissed at me? I mean what was I to do he tried to kill me and he was a vampire. Chris is a vampire? What did she mean that she tried to kill me? Why did she want to do that? She is pissed at me. Bloody vampire! I drank too much that is it. I will wake up in a hung over state tomorrow still living in the east. This was just one weird black out or something. Why did she have to be a vampire! I wonder if she likes or liked garlic on her food?

Chapter 14

The next night Christine got up and decided to go out and grab a bite to eat. She went a couple of blocks away by foot. There stood a bar and grill like there does in every city. She ordered some pasta, and she sat at the bar drinking beer, trying to watch a football game. She finished her meal with a just a few interruptions from some of the local patrons, mostly men. She decided there, somewhere between the salad and a thought, that she would head out to the strip and try not to think about her situation. She paid her bill and was out the door back to her abode to make herself over. She took a shower and as she slipped out to dry herself off the doorbell rang. Not really thinking about it she went to the door and opened it to find Leif standing there.

"I think we have some problems to work out eh Chris."

"I did expect to see you again, or at least so soon."

"Do you mind if I come in?"

"Not at all."

"Well I have no idea on how to bring this up but lets see…"

"I cannot believe you are a werewolf and you did not tell me!" Christine screamed into my ear.

"Me!? I cannot believe you were the one that was sucking on my neck the other night."

"Hey, you do not know how hard that was for me. You have no idea the pressure I am under. And now that you are a werewolf, hell I did not know you even existed I thought we were the only myths that were true. This is like some weird freak show B rated movie."

"Wait a minute you did not know about us?"

"No, why should I have?"

"Well let me put it this way. The pressure you thought you were under has just raised exponentially. We are not in a good situation by any means."

"I know! Here I go and fall in love with what I presumed was a man that turned out to be a werewolf. I mean explain that."

"You are in love with me?"

"What, oh well to let everything out into the open. Yes! Yes I am in love with you Leif."

"Oh boy," Scratching my head I fumble for a smoke. Moving into the living room, "This is where it gets complicated."

"Why?"

"Well I figured since I knew I loved you but did not know exactly how you felt. I could just dump ya and we could both go our separate ways. I

Never Fall in Love with a Vampire. It is a Pain in the Neck

figure hell I would get over you in a couple of decades at the worst a century. But now I don't want to go."

"I do not want you to go."

I plopped on Chris' couch and lit up the smoke. Scratching my nose in frustration, Chris joined me with her head on my shoulders.

"Leif. The thing I am a part of is complex. More are coming now because of last night. In fact they are probably here now trying to find me to get answers. They will want to know about you. No one kills one of us and gets away with it."

"Yea, I figured something like this would happen. That is why I called some of my friends to come here and help."

"What are we going to do about this?"

"I was hoping you had some ideas."

"I know that you should stay away from me. When I can get away I will see you then but for the next couple of days heed my words Leif."

"That is fine, not to worry about my friends. I only called the ones that would be somewhat sympathetic to this here thing."

"If they are you friends then I am not worried."

"I wish I could say the same but frankly I am scared shitless."

"Honestly Leif, you should be. I have little control over these matters; we are somewhat a feudalistic system."

We sat on the couch for awhile not saying anything just watching the bustling of the L.A. migrants. Looking for the devil to deign on our existence instead of waiting for revelation to save us from it. Bodies held in the night for as long as I could until my time came calling on other matter. I lifted my head off of Chris' lap and made ready. Leaving the comfort of the here and now for the part in the next act.

"We will get through this, after all these years some tolerance has to have come between our kinds." I said.

"What do you mean by all of that?"

"I should be going, it is getting late and there are some weirdos out there." Realizing she has to get got up on her history.

"Wait what do you mean." Christine confused now.

"Ask one of yours, then I will tell you what I know."

"But..."

"Good night Chris, see you soon. It is better to hear it from them."

I walked out the door as she watched me go down the hallway. I hit button on the elevator and the door opened. I stepped in and turned around to see her at her door.

I grinned, "You really love me don't you?"

"Oh I guess so." Smiling shyly.

"You must be weird." Feeling my libido growing. I blew her a kiss as the door shut.

Never Fall in Love with a Vampire. It is a Pain in the Neck

Chapter 15

I left the apartments for the beach, back to Charlie's to meet some old friends. I grabbed a taxi and directed him unto the restaurant slash bar. I was filled with a calming joy not just about Chris but I was to see my friends. I wonder who was going to be there and who was taking their time to get to L.A. I wonder what they have been up to, where they have been, who they have been. We passed the roads, highways, byways, cars, buses as the airplanes flew overhead. The night air was fresh and delightful as my smiled formed onto my face. I watched everyone on the way there thinking of friends and long lost times. We finally arrived and threw the cabbie a little extra as I wanted to spread the anticipation of good fortune. I stepped out onto the parking lot and walked into the bar. I greeted Charlie and looked around the bar. "No one ah well I am early." I sat at the bar.

"Hey Charlie, how are ya?"

"Not bad Leifer." Charlie smiled as he brought me a beer.

"I am glad to hear it."

"And how are you my young friend?"

"I ain't that young Charlie, but I do well." Smiling as I lit up a smoke.

"And the woman?"

I grinned "You know Charlie, I am always in trouble with women."

"Ha, somehow I don't believe you I mean about the plural part."

"Oh come Charlie I am a player just the like rest of us."

"Sure you are and I do not like beer!"

"Ok you got me, but I am in trouble with this one."

"Ah Leifer it can't be that bad eh what is the problem?"

"Not tonight Charlie, I am awaiting some old friends and we are gonna get rowdy with you in here tonight."

"No stripping tonight, Leifer."

"You just won't let that go will ya." Laughing.

"Is this guy giving you a hard time." A stranger with a familiar voice echoes behind me.

I turn to see three gentlemen looking worn and ragged. The odd ball group: a small stocky man wearing cutoff jeans and a T-shirt, a taller middle age man whom spoke with a grin from a beard and glasses, the third was a lanky character clean cut in khakis. They all posed their character to the bar as Jimmy, the smaller, lit a smoke.

"Now you see these guys Charlie, they are what you would describe as hooligans." I shot them a smile as I got up to approach them.

Chris Crase

The professor received me first with a hug. "Leif you son of a bitch, how long has it been!"

"Oh man at least fifteen years. Scotty how in the hell are ya?"

"All right." Scotty bashed away with a flimsy handshake.

"Jimmy I see you are still a runt. When are ya gonna grow?"

"Hey I am tall enough to give you a swift kick in the arse."

"Come let us get a table." I motioned to the back of the bar were the sea breeze would reach us from the porch.

That night as the world passed us by without care we bellowed, howled, cheered, and laughed over our past years without each other. Jimmy who is a drifter told us of the past seven years in Canada. Nights he chased a stripper while being chased by Mounties. The cold winters in one town or another with another girl each time. Scotty spent most of his time in Minneapolis working as a coffee shop employee, writing away on science fiction books that he never tried to publish. He was up to thirty-two books. The Professor as we nicknamed him has a place for runaways in Seattle. Tim, my best friend was in Chicago trying to close a deal before making his way out west. Always the banker, Timmy is.

"So what is the deal Tim is working on?" I inquired.

"You know Tim, this is always the one that is gonna put him in retirement."

"His head is always dreaming of fast cars and faster women."

"Here here to that!" Jimmy shouts.

"So what about you Prof how are your kids?"

"They are perfect. I love my job; the people are awesome and we are really making differences in these kids. The only misfit that we are having problems with reminds me of you, Leif and of course let me not forget Jimmy."

"We are a pain in the arse aren't we?" Jimmy smirks.

"Hey what time is it?" Scotty inquires.

"Ahh, there is no need to ask that question tonight!" I heckled.

"I am just wondering cause we are the only one who are in this place and it has been that way for the last half an hour."

Scotty was right. It was 2:30 in the morning and Charlie was just finishing cleaning up the rest of the bar. He motioned me over so I decided that it was a good time for the bathroom too.

"Hey Leifer I am heading home to the wife and kids so here are the keys. Help yourself to the beers and what not."

"Why thanks Charlie."

"Don't mention it these are your friends and you have to catch up right eh."

Never Fall in Love with a Vampire. It is a Pain in the Neck

"You are a good man Charlie."

"Just don't tell my wife." Charlie, grinning, slaps me on the shoulder.

I returned from the bathroom to see my comrades mood had shifted from good times to the problem which I invited them into. I pulled up my seat and took a slug of beer into my system. Scotty looked at the Prof and Jimmy for them to start the conversation.

The Prof took initiative. "So Leif we all know that there is a problem so what is it?"

"Vampires." I lit smoke.

Jimmy interjected "Vampires! Oh shit man they are here?"

"Yep."

The Prof trying to calm the tension, "What happened?"

"I killed one." I took a drink then another.

"Oh man that is a problem, what happened?" Scotty spoke up.

"He mistook me for dinner one night and I took care of it."

Jimmy lifted his glass to me, "Good for you Leif, those bastards just can't leave well enough alone."

I did not toast Jimmy instead I went to the bar a retrieved four more drinks. The Prof sensing more let the other two bicker until I returned. I looked at him and could sense that I needed to come clean.

"All right there is more" Jimmy and Scotty stopped and looked at me for the more. "There is a bigger problem than that my friends. The reason the vampire tried to kill me was well how can I put this… It was over a woman."

"A woman?" Scotty stated "That is not such a big deal."

Frustrated I let it out "A vampire woman Jimmy."

The Prof knowing where this was heading sat back a grabbed one of my smokes.

"What did you try to kill her too?" Jimmy asked.

"No."

"I don't understand." Scotty confused.

"You are in love with her aren't you Leif?" the Prof spoke.

"Yes."

"What in the hell are you talking about." Jimmy was getting very edgy.

"It is simple, I met a girl who turned out to be a vampire. We fell in love. She was ordered to kill me and when she couldn't this guy Jarred the other vampire tried to and that is when I killed him."

"Why in the hell do you want to love one of those bastards."

"I love her not what she turned out to be. It is not like I planned it but I really do not care what she is other than her."

The Prof spoke again "So Leif how do you want to handle this?"

Chris Crase

"That is why I brought you here, I do not know what to do."

"What do you mean of course you know what to do just walk away from it. Tell her goodbye or not and just leave. Don't make trouble Leif." Jimmy spoke up.

"I concur Leif." Scotty stated "We don't need this."

"And you Prof?"

"I can't tell you what to do, I know you better than Scotty and Jimmy so they do not appreciate it as much as I do but I would have to say it is up to you. We will be behind you no matter what."

"I love her."

"Does she love you."

"Yes."

"Are you sure."

"With all my heart."

"Then it looks like we are staying awhile in L.A."

"What do you mean we are staying here? This is no good." Jimmy stated.

"Leif needs our help."

"Yeah, but this is not about a bunch of punks nor financial troubles. We are going to be getting into a mess that I thought ended over a thousand years ago. Sure there were a couple of instances among those years but not like this. I mean you killed one of them and they are not gonna take that lightly. Hell the stuff I have heard about when a human takes one theirs. They are ruthless. I cannot even imagine what they want to do to you. Leif you are asking us to forget the past and help you fight for one of those bastards."

"She doesn't even know about that."

"Oh now since she is a little naive I am suppose to trust her."

"I am asking you to trust me."

"Hey Leif believe me I am your friend and I would walk through hell and back. But you are asking too much. What the vampires did to us a thousand some odd years ago is inexcusable and we fought and won now you are asking us to risk that all again cause this is gonna be big."

"I never said it was going to be easy."

"I am sorry but I cannot help you."

"I understand Jimmy, I will see you when it is over."

"Leif, don't push this I am asking you to walk away from her."

"Cannot do that."

"Damnit you are so infuriating, Leif. I am outta here. Good luck."

"Bye Jimmy."

Never Fall in Love with a Vampire. It is a Pain in the Neck

"Scotty are you going to stay? I can tell the Prof is going to help out this lunatic."

"I have to agree with Jimmy on this one Leif. It is just too much trouble." Scotty informing me and the Prof.

"All right it looks like it is me and you, Prof."

"Good bye guys." Scotty gets up, "It was good seeing you again Leif."

Scotty and Jimmy took off into the night. Jimmy complaining his side all the way out the door as Scotty was strolling around him. The Prof and I got another drink. And sat back down.

"Hey Leif don't let Jimmy get to you. He just can't let it go."

"I know I know, what about you?"

"Me hell I cannot let it go either and believe me if was anyone else I would be out that door in a second. But I am your friend and if it is important as you say it is then I will be behind you all the way. As for those two, they are not leaving town for awhile. They will probably see how the rest of us react to it first."

"Speaking of which do you think you could get Marcus to do something?"

"Ah I do not know. He was there when all the shit went down."

"I know but if we could get him to change his mind. I mean hell how long can both of our kinds ignore each other? They have to be somewhat tolerant of us. Maybe someone in there group."

"You are asking a lot but if we could get Marcus on our side we might be able to get them to back down."

"I just cannot believe we can be so prejudice against them anymore nor them to us. Well okay I did not really care for them cause I never had any trouble with them but then this wonderful person walks into my life and..."

"Hey Leif I need no further convincing."

"Sorry."

"It is all right, I will try tomorrow to get a message to Marcus."

"Thanks Prof."

"And I am gonna have a talk to our two friends too."

"Good hopefully Timmy will be here soon and he can help ya."

"So where is this lady, I would like to meet her."

"Me and her have decided to lay low and she will get a hold of me when she feels it is safe for me."

"That is probably a good idea. Knowing them they already have a flock forming here."

"I just hope they have some like you on their side."

"Me too Leif, me too."

"So do have a place to stay?"

Chris Crase

"Yeah, I have a place up the coast about twenty miles."

"Good that is near here and I am here a lot. Come on I will bring you to your hotel."

"Sounds good."

After I dropped off the Prof, I took a drive further up north. It was rather a dead drive until dawn hit and people started their daily commutes. I pulled off the side of the road to watch the sun come over the east and strike the ocean. I sat there watching the waves make their way into the coves. I drove further until I hit a town. I stopped for breakfast. Over coffee and eggs and burnt toast I studied my books. Not really caring but somehow trying to get my mind off my life and her. I left the restaurant and wandered around this sleepy town. Jumping cracks in the sidewalk while the sun beat down on me. I thought about what Jimmy said, maybe he was right. Why should I go making trouble for us? Who was I to do this? Just a drifter who was given a chance at living an eternity doing all that I wanted. Exploiting life with all its shortcomings, I was a god at living. I was an actor, an engineer, a philosopher, now a doctor, a trucker, and owner of numerous shops along the way, a cook, and even no one at the same time. My life was good, and now I have to fall in love. The only thing I never thought I would do in my life. Yet I cannot imagine going on in life without ever being with her. Who are we to place our names among Romeo and Juliet, Portos and Madeline, Marc and Cleo. We are just two crazy kids. Somehow through my wanderings I ended back at my car and the diner. I took off back to the city. I drove back thinking of nothing in particular just annoying other drivers with my renditions of classic rock.

Chapter 16

That night Christine awoke feeling uneasy; she put on a dress and was off to the strip where she first met Leif. She walked into the bar to see the same old character that hit on her that particular night. He was more sober and still drunk with his cockiness, and as she past him and his group of twins he grinned at her and then proceeded to watch her ass as she made her way to the bar.

Christine thought to herself "Doesn't this guy have another wardrobe?"

The bartender came over and retrieved her order. She sat back and watched the setting unfold around her. For a weeknight the place was rather busy and loud. Girls dressed up like her with some boyfriends who can't take the initiative to dance with their dates so the girls head out and bump it with other men. Meanwhile the boyfriends in a jealous rage sit in a deaden state until the other guy gets too friendly which usually resulted in the men leaving there seats to reclaim there girlfriends in a groping frenzy on the floor. As she watched the social ritual continue, Christine felt a tap on her shoulder. It was the player whom obviously did not remember her.

"Hey there, how is it going?" as he runs his eyes over her body.

Not really in the mood of belittling Christine mutters "Not bad and you."

In an effort to be in control he looks at a group of girls at the end of the bar. "I am doing all right." Looking back at her. "So what are you doing here by yourself?"

"I am waiting for my friend."

He grins, "And who might that be." assuredly cause he has heard that line before. He motions to the bartender.

"Oh he is my best friend."

Breaking her sentence "So what are you drinking?"

"Vodka gimlet."

"That sounds good, I'll take one too."

The bartender hears the order and runs to make it as Christine lights up a smoke.

"So you are?"

"James, and you?"

"Christine."

He nods in understanding while the bartender hands his drink to him and motions to James two dollars. James pulls out a brassy money clip filled with ones and pulls out two dollars. He folds them between his index and middle finger and hands them to the barkeep.

Chris Crase

"So would you like to dance?"

"Listen James," Getting a little annoyed, "I am really waiting for a friend and I really do not feel like being bothered."

"It is your lost, baby."

"Not by the looks of it."

"Little miss pretentious, eh? That is fine by me there are a dozen of women like you in here tonight so don't think you are all that."

"Why not you think that you are all that."

"I am."

"Oh really!" Christine strikes a grin, "So being all that means getting women drunk and basically using them because you are physically attractive and dress the latest styles."

"What the hell are you talking about?"

"Nothing this conversation is over."

Christine turns cheek to the other side of the bar. James picks up his drink and begins to walk away flicking his hand at Christine in a gesture of forget you as he murmurs "Bitch" in attempt to save face with his friends. On his way back to his friends, three gents confront him. One of them was a well built man in his late twenties maybe early thirties with a devilish goatee and brown hair. The other two were twins: one well dressed and the other kinda mangled also in the same age group with blond hair.

"Are you giving the lady a problem?" Asked the non-twin.

"Hey, that bitch has majors problems."

"That bitch is a friend."

The two twins move around the speaker to encircle James.

"Hey, I do not want any trouble I just want to get back to my friends at the table."

"Go and get your friends and get out." As the man walks through James to Christine. Turning around James again tries to save face with a confronting look. The twins still looking him dead in the eye make James change his mind. He scurries back to the table and tells his friends to leave.

"Hello Christine."

Christine looks to see her old friend, "Morgan, I knew you would come."

"Well, the council wanted to send others but I convinced them to send me since I know you better."

"So what have you heard, and who are your friends?"

"These are Jean and Lucas, the council requested that they come with me." Morgan waves the bartender over to get some drinks for him and his friends. "Three drafts please."

"Well?"

Never Fall in Love with a Vampire. It is a Pain in the Neck

"All we have heard is that Jarred was killed, you know something about it."

The barkeep returns and Christine gets another drink and proceeds to light a cigarette. "You are going to find out anyway so I will just tell you. Jarred was killed by my boyfriend."

"Did you deal with him."

"He is my boyfriend."

"We both know we can't keep relationships with humans."

"You did not let me finish."

"Okay."

"My boyfriend, after I tried to kill him once on Jarred's orders and after Jarred tried to kill him once, that makes twice for all those paying attention, proceeded to turn into a werewolf and rip him to pieces."

The two twins hearing this let out disgusted looks at Christine. Morgan feeling the talk getting a little more serious tried to mediate.

"That does become a problem, one that might not be so easily rectified."

"So where is your boyfriend at now?" Asked Lucas the ruffian.

"How do I know. I haven't spoke to him since that incidence."

"He must die." announced Jean.

"Yes, he does" Morgan iterated, "Lucas, Jean leave us and contact the ones on the west coast and get them down here as soon as possible. Then let the council know the situation. We will meet tomorrow and make preparations for our friends."

Jean and his brother slam their beers and leave the bar to act on Morgan's orders and to feed on some Californian's afterwards. Morgan pulls up the stool next to Christine and asks for a smoke.

"So how have you been, Christine? What has it been fifty? Sixty years?"

"At least, I have been doing well. Let's see I have spent most of that time just hopping around the States with a few excursions to the old country."

"You have been staying away from us."

"Yeah, well I had to get out on my own." Christine smiles "You forget I still am a rebellious teenager."

"Yep, I know that you have always been a pain in my rear."

"Oh, come on not always."

"All right not always, so how long have you been in LA?"

"Just a couple of months."

"And how long have you know this guy. What is his name?"

"Leif, oh just a little bit shorter than that."

"And how long have you been in love with him."

Chris Crase

"What do you mean?'

"Come on Christine, I know you like no one else. You know where he is, you have seen him since he killed Jarred, you know that no one will understand and that is why you are protecting him."

"Am I right though?"

"For the most part yes, as for me you will have to convince me but I will listen."

"Well, I want to listen first."

"Okay, what can I tell you?"

"What is the deal between us and them."

"He did not tell you?"

"He told me to ask you."

"I like him already."

"So what happened."

Chapter 17

Marcus awoke that morning in his chambers much as he always did. Opening the shudders to his room he peered out over the countryside to see the sun striking the distant villages in the valley. Dressing himself in his peasant clothes and washing up, he began to prepare for his daily chores as every day before that and to come. The bed of the room held his clothes that were worn out of days. Marcus retreated to pick them up with his hands, like his clothes his hands were torn and aged with scars of work. He eyed his stone fingers as they tried to fell the softness of the fibers in the shirt as the sunlight tried to warm the dead palms. Numbness of life had taken the place of touch from his hands, body. He looked upon the sun and imagined the warmth of light on his skin to remind him of younger days. This was his way of preparing for the day.

He scampered down the stairs to the kitchen where the other workers of the castle were gathering. He helped the women prepare the table for him and the other men. He helped them every day among the ridicule of his fellow males. It was due to this young vixen that worked in the kitchen named Sophia. She stole his heart a few years back and the only way to express his feeling toward her was to help her with her morning regiment of preparing the food for everyone. As he set the table he would occasionally glance up to catch a glimpse of her at the other end setting the silverware. They had a nice arrangement of her setting the silverware and he proceeded with the plates.

Moments later the men came in from conversing in the hallway and seated themselves to be served. At the table it was the usual conversation of moans and groans: the cows were sick, the cages for the hens were falling apart, another dog ran off, the carriage broke again. Every morning the same talk and the same outcome, except for Logan. Logan was considered to be an elder but was somewhere in between. He sat there eating he breakfast quietly and self-contained. Every now and then he was bothered for his help in some one chores which he would assuredly assist. Marcus would wonder sometimes with Sophia about what Logan thought about all the time but really was only an excuse for Marcus to talk to Sophia.

After the meal, the women would emerge to clear the table and make way for them to eat their morning's effort while the men took to the outdoors. Each of them had a responsibility to fulfill before the lords awoke, some would attend the livestock while others went to the towns to trade and get daily gossip, and Logan and Marcus took out the dead. They went to the great hall and the lord's secondary bedrooms to fetch the corpses

Chris Crase

of the villagers. The duty had its ups and downs, today was an up. There was only one body of an old man in the great hall which all the lords feasted on. Ridding the castle of the old was easy to do, especially with only one. Logan and Marcus wrapped him in the spare linen and cleaned up the blood stained table. They dragged him out into the courtyard and placed him into the trailer and went and made ready the horses. After hitching the horses, the two proceeded to one of the towns where the old man was not from. Sometimes the duty is worse. Sometimes the lords will get over zealous and leave Logan and Marcus with five sometimes seven people who were mostly young. These were the situations when the two coroners had to be clever. It would require an entire day of running all over the countryside placing a couple at various body dumps they chose for the isolation, others would be clawed and mangled and left in a common hunting ground, and others like today would have their throats slit and belongs tossed in the river. Today, Logan and Marcus took the body to a town and give the locals the story of finding this poor man along the road dead. Today was an up day for them. They would be back in time to help the others tackle bigger projects that would come along today, everyday.

After giving the locals the body, they proceeded to a pub to hear the news of the day to inform the lords of certain events and what not. As they sat there Marcus would carry on the conversations which he had come quite affluent in as Logan just sat thinking and analyzing the folks. Logan would participate only when Marcus had too much to drink and begin to assert his masculinity over the locals. The only other times Logan would converse with people would be when he discovered they were travelers from a great distances or scholars. Though these efforts Logan had learned to read and write over the years and was becoming quite a learned individual without anyone, even Marcus, knowing. Today there was only the news of the annual festival where villages from all over would come to celebrate one the countries many upheavals which resulted in usually a massacre of idealist and people longing for freedom against the aristocrats and bourgeois. Marcus forgot about all the occasion but was quickly reminded when he saw the square and courtyards being decorated for the arrival and celebration of friends and families. Logan, however, did not forget as he paraded the town with a gloom heart and heavy head. For he knew the next few days would be busy for him and Marcus. He drooped along over cobblestone and dust that had fallen the night before looking at the gay and proud people of the village.

Marcus came up to Logan in the street and informed him of the time and that they should depart. Logan looked at him and agreed and they proceeded to the horses. On the way down the streets they passed a bathhouse. Logan looked at it as they passed it and stopped and stared at it as Marcus continued on. A few moments later when Marcus realized his ramblings where falling on only his own ears he turned around to look at Logan.

"What are you doing?" as he reproached Logan.

Logan, without turning away from the front door, said "Lets go in and take comfort in the warm baths, Marcus."

"What?! We don't have time for that."

"Why not?"

"Cause we have to get back and help with the chores."

"But ours are done."

"We have to help the others before the lords awake."

"They will be done and besides the lords have other things to worry about tonight than making sure all the chores are done."

"Well, then where are we going to get the money for the baths?'

Logan pulls out his pouch and retrieves his savings.

Marcus stunned "Where did you get that!?"

"Every now and then I sneak a few from the change we get from supplies and it just builds up."

"If the lords knew about this we would be locked down for a month and never allowed to venture outside the castle again."

"They do not know though."

"But we cannot, I have to help out preparing dinner."

"I am sure Sophia will not mind missing one time of you gazing over her with nothing to say to her."

Blushing, Marcus again stands firm "If the lords knew..."

"They will not know..." Logan grabbing Marcus' arm, "Let us go inside."

Logan led Marcus up the stairs and into the bathhouse. He paid for both of them to enter the public baths where the villagers were enjoying a weekly routine of relaxing and cleaning their worked bodies. Attendants eagerly sought to Logan's and Marcus' clothes and gave them towels. They emerge from changing rooms to see a large steaming pool of mineral water. Smaller pools were set off to the side some of them were VIP and others were filled with warm mud with warm waters falling from behind them to wash off the therapeutic dirt.

Grinning at the blanked face Marcus, Logan darted to one of the mud pools. Marcus hurried behind him. They both stood at the rim of the grayish muck, hesitantly Logan proceed in and sat down.

"Ahh, wonderful, absolutely wonderful." as he laid back his head and closed his eyes.

Chris Crase

"Is it hot?"

"Hot?! it is magnificent, come in Marcus."

Marcus took a big heave and cautiously entered.

Laughing, Logan stated "Now this is living. Marcus, you should not be so nervous."

"I just do want to get in trouble."

"How can we get in trouble here?"

"I mean back at the castle, everyone will be upset with us."

"Oh, Marcus, just enjoy the moment and worry about that when it comes."

"But…"

"Marcus, I do not want to here another 'but' out of you today."

"But…"

"Marcus…"

"All right, I will just sit here."

"That is right, sit there and feel the goodness of the mud."

"It does feel pretty good."

"I told you." Logan grinning with his eyes shut.

Logan and Marcus spent the rest of the afternoon soaking their bodies in the health waters of the bathhouse. They talked and mused about people of the castle, and they swam the warm pools forgetting their roles in life. Emerging from the bathhouse, the newly renovated looked toward the west to see the sun beginning to set as well as reality. They hurried to the horses and made off to the castle; they might make it back in time for dinner and they hoped before the lords awoke. Marcus began to show his uneasiness as they rushed home as Logan tried to remain as composed as he could. Marcus chattered all the way back about their stupidity of the day and how everyone, especially the lords, would be upset at them if they found out. Logan tried to reassure him to just keep it quiet and not to mention it to any one not even Sophia. Marcus said he would make the effort.

Never Fall in Love with a Vampire. It is a Pain in the Neck

Chapter 18

Arriving at the castle gates, they saw their fellow workers putting away their tools and readying themselves for dinner. As Logan and Marcus began to strip the mounts and put away the horses, they received queries from some of their friends. Marcus kept quiet as Logan explained that they had some trouble with the locals where they brought the body. With that excuse the friends became more inquisitive fearing the local village might be on to their masters, but Logan reasserted himself and explained that the situation was under control.

As the men fell onto the dining table, the gossip had reached the inside help. Sophia kept eyeing Marcus with concern and all young Marcus could do was ignore the whole dinner and sit quietly at the table allowing Logan to control the explanations. With dinner progressing, Logan began to grow wearisome of his elaborate excuse and was almost ready to give in when the sound of commotion in the castle silenced the workers. The lords had awoke and began their preparations for the night. The workers sat listening to the lords assembling in the hall to make ready their own festivities tonight. Each of the workers awaited for the sound of the main door creak open and the flutter of the winds as they lifted the lords into the night. Despair set over the group as they regained their focus and Logan peered across the lot.

"Well now," Logan broke the silence, "I guess we should prepare to turn in for the night for tomorrow will be a long day."

The men removed themselves to allow the women to see after the mess and they proceeded to stoke the fires and prepare the main hall for their lords return. That night would be hard to sleep with the extraordinary ruckus that will soon begin. And so the cycle continues. Aching, Logan made his way to his abode, he approached the one of the back stairs that led him home. Looking down he could almost see the albatrosses on each foot as he slowly ascended the steps. In his room he sat down and paused before he took off his boots. Day in and day out, he took off the left boot followed by the right. Every night he sat on his bed slowly taking off his shirt that hung loosely over the shoulders that had been molding to carry dead villagers. Each eve, he poured a glass of water and waited till the first scream to come from inside the castle. Then he could go to sleep.

The next couple of months the chores were done day in and day out. Sophia and Marcus where becoming very close and would sometimes sneak away during the day to take a few short walks. At night she would brave the corridors to make her way to his chambers. Logan seemed to become more

Chris Crase

depressed as each day dragged on but only noticeable to Marcus. Marcus, however, paid no real attention to him as he was busy with happiness. But each day they took the bodies from the castle. One particular day as Logan and Marcus were burying and young vagabond in the wood, Logan broke the usual conversation.

"Have you noticed how Lord Haden is particularly vicious with these humans?"

"Huh,what do you mean?" Marcus taken off guard.

"Well look at this man." Logan pointed to the leg of the nomad, "These are Haden's marks here and since he has grown in power in the castle so has his viciousness with each victim."

"Oh, I had not noticed." Marcus now taking an interest in the marks over the body, "So who are these teeth marks on the chest?"

"Lord Drake's, he is always found of the chest area, and those on the right arm are Mistress Drake's. She takes the arms of males and the necks of women. She is very particular."

"And these all over the back of the legs?"

"Those are the marks over the lowers vampires."

"Really."

"Yes, they get seconds and usually go for the legs cause that is where the rest of the blood seems to reside after the lords have taken theirs."

"Why are you so interested in the bodies, Logan?"

"Well, you know I guess the job is just getting to me. These are people, Marcus, why do they deserve this fate? I mean we hunt as well sometimes but only the creatures of the forest we never take the human's life why should our lords?"

"Because that is how it has been."

"Yes, but does Haden have to be so vicious?"

"Logan have you seen what he does when they take one of us."

"No."

"Haden is worse than what you see here when they take one of us."

"Really."

"The night when the lords felt like taking August, I saw it."

"What did you see?"

"Well I was running late with my chores and the lords were in the great hall and I guess they were depressed if you say about the quality of the humans blood the night before. So they saw August making his rounds stoking the fires and Haden decided to take him. August tried to resist but as soon as the lords tasted his blood they were ravishing him. He could not do anything and Haden was well..."

"Haden was what?'

Never Fall in Love with a Vampire. It is a Pain in the Neck

"Well it looked like he was almost having fun with it."

"I can't believe that."

"Believe it Logan but that is the way of it. They are the lords and we must obey."

By this time the two were walking back to the castle and the rest of the workers were busy with the chores. The sun was about to break the horizon on the western slope as it warmed the backs of the two walking through the gate. Logan went his separate way to help out the others while Marcus went to clean and store their tools. And so when the sun was half empty the workers went to have dinner. Talk was abounding tonight for the full moon was out and that meant the lords allowed the hunt for the workers. As of late though the workers just used it as an excuse to gather outside the castle free of their bond. The night would usually consist of fire, howls, and wine. Logan seemed to be particular fond of these nights. After cleaning and preparing the dwellings for the masters, the workers left through the main gate. The young ones took off in a fluent run through the woods as the elders followed. The young workers hurried to prepare the campsite with wood and a fire while the elders carried the food and wine to the site. As the elders approached the campsite they split apart so not to notice each other's transformation. The campsite was ablaze with a fire as the young ones retreated into the darkened rim of the woods to transform themselves.

Moments later the blackness started to flutter with silver as the fire and moonlight emitted from the fur. The shadows of silver began to approach the fire and as the group emerged life began for only a night. The eldest, Corina, walked to the fire as the rest of the workers hunched over watched her. She stopped and picked up a flask of wine and turned to the pack; each one eagerly waiting. With one great heave she let out the howl to start the night. The others proceeded to join in the call of wild lost. A scrappy young worker took to the others as the playful fighting began. The elders sat down and watched the wrestling. The females fetched the rest of the flasks and joined the elders.

Logan sat with the elders watching young Marcus leave the playing to join Sophia and another young female. Logan sat still watching Marcus make a fool of himself as the other young males kept nagging him from the swaree.

Logan shouted over to Marcus to participate in the roast, "Marcus, see what happens when you grow up and leave the friends behind for a pretty face."

The males began to laugh as Marcus tucked his tail at the comment.

Laughing Logan continued, "Don't worry Marcus, Sophia will appreciate the fool you are becoming."

Chris Crase

With that Marcus pounced Logan and pushed him to the ground and said "'Tis I the fool to try or are you the fool for standing on the outside laughing at me?"

"Good point." Logan tosses Marcus with his superior strength., and throws his paws on to Marcus' head and submits him, "But right now it seems that you are still the fool."

Marcus strains in vain to free himself, as the rest of the wolves laugh at his misfortunes. Logan keeps a smirk with his fangs as he displays his kill. Looking over to the elders for their approving laugh, Logan is blindsided by Sophia. Logan yips at the shock which send the pack into a louder howl of laughter. Logan dusts himself off turning to Sophia.

Sophia grins at him "Now who is the fool for letting a young girl take him."

Grinning, Logan looks to Marcus "You better hold onto this one Marcus she is quite the bitch."

Marcus gets up and pushes out his chest "That is right you mess with me and you got to mess with her." as he addresses the young males and proceeds to a flask of wine.

Logan sits back down with the elders with a large grin. He picks up a flask of wine and proceeds to catch a gulp of wine and the playing and howling continues. His attention gets diverted as he hears three elders talk about the chores. He begins to listen attentively as the two moan to the other about how their work is slipping which is going to lead to a backlash from the lords. The later begins to refer to one of his punishments from years ago when it took him an extra day to fix the carriage wheel. With this Logan joins into the conversation.

"Do you know what I and Marcus did some months ago when we went to a town."

The three look at him with a 'this is our conversation' look, "What did you do?" One of them asks.

"We spent the day in a local bath house."

A few more elders caught the statement and joined in the group.

"What were you thinking, Logan you could have received some serious repercussions from doing that. Where did you get the money for that anyway?"

"I stole it. Here and there from the lords."

"What!" a few of the elders say.

"Listen." Logan perches himself on a log. "It was one of the best things that we ever did. I coaxed young Marcus away from our duties to go and enjoy ourselves for once."

"Yes, but we cannot go off and..."

Never Fall in Love with a Vampire. It is a Pain in the Neck

"And what? Live for ourselves? Have the freedom to go and do what we want when we will."

"What are you saying Logan?"

"I am saying I am tired of being a worker for the lords. I want to go and..."

"And what? Work for a human?"

"...I want the chance to go and travel if I want. I want to be able to say that I am not getting up today. I want to see the world. I want..."

"That is being selfish Logan" Coriana jumps in. "We have a responsibility as do the rest scattered around at different castles and towns. This is how it has been since the beginning. The lords gave us a chance when we did not know who we were and lacked continuity, and we repay them by serving them."

"Well maybe we know who we are now and it is not this."

"What are going to do Logan?" Coriana becoming defensive, "Lead a revolt kill the lords? You will never win, they are too strong."

"But we are strong too if we do it together."

"No, they are too strong." another elder steps in.

"But we can try."

"Try what, there is nothing to try."

"Our life is nothing?"

"The lords treat us well and we will continue on this path."

Coriana speaks again "Logan just stop this right now other wise you will be getting the lot of us in trouble that we do not want."

"If you say so Coriana." Logan sits back down and watches the fire.

"It is getting to be day break soon we should go back." Coriana states.

The pack begins to disappear into the wood to transform back into workers. Walking back to the dwellings to start the day, Logan took the way back along the stream as the others stayed together talking and moaning about their work that lied ahead of them. Marcus made his way from the rest of them to find Logan. He saw him sitting on the rock watching dawn approach over the hills.

"Why did you tell the others about the bathhouse!" exclaimed Marcus. "We said that we were keeping that to ourselves."

"I just wanted to let them know that there lies something outside of our work."

"Yeah, trouble."

"Oh, come on, what trouble?"

"The lords, you know."

"Marcus."

"What."

Chris Crase

"Would you want to take that day back?"

"What do you mean."

"Well if the lords did find out would you have wished that you never did it."

"I don't understand."

"Would you rather have that day back and so it never happened, instead that day just consisted of us dropping off the body and going back to the castle and continue on."

"No, I want to do that every day."

"Even if you got in trouble"

"NO!!"

"So as long as you don't feel the consequences it is alright."

"That is what I am inferring."

"Alright, well I am sorry for letting out our secret then."

"Oh, that is okay I have been wanting to tell Sophia for the longest time, now I have something to talk to her about."

"Come on Marcus we have chores to do."

The two friends made their way to the castle where there would assuredly be work for them. And when they opened the door to the great hall they say three bodies lying on the floor. They easily identified Haden's victim as Marcus went to get some linen and Logan retrieved a bucket of water and some rags. And the day proceeded.

That night after the dinner was served and the workers were preparing for bed, Sophia made her way to the chambers of Marcus. She wandered past the lighted corridors to the north wing where Marcus resided. Sophia had to be careful for she had to pass the chambers that where set up for the lords to take their victims. Especially on the way back from his room when the lords were busily at task, the young girl's nerves were stretched. Up the flight of stairs leading to the north wing and around the corner to the hallway to where Marcus is awaiting, she slipped pass the first set of doors where upon she fell upon Haden who was coming out of his second bedroom. Haden was a tall, handsome lord whom by witnesses to his victims had the way with the local women. Sophia froze in fear, knowing that she and Marcus could be in trouble if their secret was exposed to the lords. Haden neatly dressed walked to her with an inquisitive look on his strong, sharp face.

"And where are you off to in this side of the castle, young thing?"

"I was off to see about Marcus, my lord."

"Sophia, is it not?"

"Yes my lord."

Never Fall in Love with a Vampire. It is a Pain in the Neck

Haden sweeps over her young body with his eyes and inquires, "So what is the problem with our young Marcus?"

"Oh, well he did not dinner tonight and I was fearing that he might be ill."

"That is very considerate of you Sophia, please do not allow me to keep you anymore. Go and see after Marcus."

"Thank you my lord" Sophia makes her way around Haden as he watches her down the hallway.

"You will of course," Haden calling after her "Keep me informed of young Marcus' condition."

"Of course, my lord." Sophia stops and turns to acknowledge him.

As soon as Sophia turned the corner, she picked up her pace to get to Marcus as quickly as possible. She knocked on his door and turned her head down the corridor which she came to se the Shadow of Haden disappear into the rest of the castle. Marcus opened the door and she quickly entered the chambers of her loved one.

"Is everything alright?" Marcus queried.

"I just ran into Lord Haden on the way here."

"Are you okay?'

"Yes, he just spooked me I guess."

"What did he want?"

"He was coming out of his bedroom and on his way out for the night. He asked me what I was doing and I said that you were ill and I was checking on you."

"Did he believe you?"

"I think so."

"Good, then there is nothing to worry about."

"I hope so I just do not like him and his smugness."

"Of course you don't like him no one does. I do not even think the other lords like him that much."

Sophia giggled, "Well that is because he has a personality of a rat."

"Oh come on the rats are not that bad."

"I guess so."

That night Sophia decided to stay with Marcus to for go in its entirety the fear of seeing Haden again. When morning came she scampered unscathed to her chambers to get cleaned for the next day of chores. And for the next few days Sophia did not make her way to the chambers of the North wing for she had the feeling of death in the air of the night corridors of seeing Haden. One night Marcus was tending the torches of the in his area when he saw Haden come to him.

"Evening Marcus."

Chris Crase

"Evening Lord Haden."

"I see that you are doing better"

"Yes thank you lord."

"Young Sophia saw to you well?"

"She is a kind worker."

"Yes she is and very sweet."

"She is a compliment to the castle my lord."

"Well Marcus I must be off to the town tonight, please if you will make a fire in my chambers. I can feel the winter coming."

"Yes, my lord."

"Good night, Marcus."

"Good night, Lord Haden."

Marcus quickly went to the lord's chambers and prepared a fire. Looking for some kindling Marcus began fishing around the chambers of Haden. He noticed that Haden a desk and hoped that he may locate some flint for the fire. Going through the drawers he noticed some rolled up papers of Haden's journal. He inquisitively sat down and looked him over. Not knowing how to read he did notice some drawings to accompany the journal entries. They were mostly of the women that Haden had seduced in his chambers. He stumbled across one of the recent entries that had a picture of Sophia in her chambers taking a bath. Wishing he knew what the words said that lay beneath his love, his hand outlined the picture. The detail of the painstakingly involved drawing amazed the young Marcus thinking of Haden's unknown talent. Very neatly, Marcus' finger traced the back of Sophia onto the curve of the bath. Smiling at the splendor in which Haden revealed the worker's love, Marcus thoughts never carried elsewhere just onto the picture of Sophia. Realizing his duties, Marcus put the journal back. He proceeded to the hallway to take a torch and lit the fire. Marcus then went to his room and awaited the chance to see Sophia.

Never Fall in Love with a Vampire. It is a Pain in the Neck

Chapter 19

That morning Marcus could not take it anymore and when he was setting the table with Sophia he begged her to come over that night. She persisted that it was not wise so Marcus settled on going to her room that night and surprising her. After breakfast, everyone continued on their daily chores and Marcus worked extra hard to finish up and return to the castle hoping that time would work just as hard as he was to bring on the night. At dinner he attentively watch Sophia serve the meals as the rest of the men carried on their usual cackle. And that night when the lords left and the torches and fires lit Marcus left his wing to the South to see his love. He cautiously made his way past Haden's chambers in case he had not left or returned early with his prize. Down the stairs into the main entry and up the staircase of the south wing. He arrived at the door and took a breath in anxiety. He opened the door quietly not to ruin the surprise and saw a dimly lit room without his love. He made his way to the other room where her bath was to see her in the warm waters but to no avail. He thought that maybe he was too persistent and she had heeded her own advice and went to his chambers. He quickly left to his room. Back down the stairs and into the main entry where he heard the vampires in the great hall. He silently made he way over and cracked the door to the hall. There he witnessed the vampires about to feed upon his beloved.

Marcus threw the door open and ran to aid Sophia whom was struggling for her life against the lower vampires. He made it about half way before Lord Drake and Lord Haden impeded his path. They seduced him to the ground as agonizing groan filled the hall. He tried to regain his feet but Mistress Drake dropped down onto his neck. He looked back at Haden who began to laugh and motion to his subjects to bring Sophia. They dragged her crying at the sight of Marcus on the ground being feasted on by the Drakes. Haden grabbed Sophia by the back of her neck he removed her clothing to reveal the young one's body to the court. He straightened his arm out holding young Sophia and gazed at the health of the female. Marcus tried to break free and have his rage fall onto the lord. He was helpless and just gazed at Sophia's trembling body as the lord looked his prize over. Indulging in the moment Haden swung around Sophia in a waltz to the court as the young lords laughed about each other as they were in a treat of two soon. Haden's eyes never left the face of Sophia during the dance. He watched her and fed off her agony as she watched her betrothed on the floor covered by his blood and the lords. As a tear left her eye that only the innocent have before the world wakes them up, Haden's eyes

Chris Crase

closed in and became engulfed onto that tear. He saw the reflection of himself in the tear and drove him into a blissful torturer. Haden then methodically brought her neck closer and closer to his mouth until his teeth pierced her white skin. As the pure blood rush into his mouth he began to feast violently on her mouth and the rest of her neck until her struggle subsisted. Sophia lost consciousness and her body went limp. Marcus screamed out as sudden as Haden was blind sided by Logan's animal.

Haden fell to the ground as the other vampires took back in astonishment. Logan wasted no time and took the initiative at keeping his adversary on the ground. Logan ripped and tore Haden's flesh with his teeth and claws. His savage growls woke the workers who began to make their footsteps louder. The Drakes wasted no time in attacking Logan. Marcus ran to Sophia being freed from their grips. Blood pouring down her and his neck, he tried to revive Sophia with futile attempts. Tears poured down as he let out a howl and looked to the lower vampires arriving at Logan. He transformed into his beast on his leapt over to them. Marcus took out two vampires and was yielding wild claw throws at anything in his path. Meanwhile, the Drakes had managed to pull away Logan from Lord Haden who was making his way to his feet gathering himself.

The workers arrived and the young ones wasted no time joining Marcus and the lower vampires. The werewolves easily outnumbered the lower vampires and quickly made them start to retreat to the other end of the hall. Pushing with every bit of rage and years of plight, the wolves left all restraint behind. The elders including Coriana watched on as Logan kept his own on the Drakes. Haden withdrew in disbelief and what he was witnessing. The final blow at the beginning of this insurrection came when the Drakes were pushing in vain Logan to the fireplace. Logan always in control of his actions and picking each blow carefully grabbed the stoker for the fire and used it throw off Lord Drake and with the same action thrusted the stoker into the heart of his mistress. She let out a shrieking cry that halted the fighting of the others. All engaged and all watching on saw in disbelief the death of a lord. Mistress Drake fell down in death as Logan stood over her in defiance to Haden who was perched high above the action. Both glared at one another, neither wincing at the other nor giving the advantage of doubt through their eyes. The hatred for each other burned their souls until the moment the watching could not bear it. The dawn was vastly approaching and the lower vampires retreated to their dungeons beneath the castle. Haden stood still with his gaze still fixed on Logan. Lord Drake made a motion to him as Drake disappeared with the others. Haden then with a smooth descent from high came down and disappeared

Never Fall in Love with a Vampire. It is a Pain in the Neck

into the darkened doorway never once breaking the stare that him and Logan engaged in.

Moments later everyone gathered around Logan and the dead mistress. The elders were clamoring with chatter at Logan and each other.

"Logan what were you thinking!?" cried one elder.

"We are all going to be punished and you Logan will be put to death"

Marcus interjected in defense of Logan, "They killed Sophia and they were going to kill me as well if it wasn't for Logan"

The elder rebutted, "Sophia's death is sad but we all know the order of things"

Logan stood still gazing over his kill as the fire burned behind him.

Once again Marcus spoke, "We broke the rules but it was for one of us"

Another elder spoke "We must make retribution and prepare for our punishment"

Logan spoke out, "No, we will do no such thing"

"What are you talking about Logan. You of us all should more sorry for your actions cause you have put us all in danger."

"I will not live like this anymore. Today we leave our bounds and never return"

"WE cannot leave, we have to work"

"Work for what? Every day we suffer for the lords and this is their way of repaying us" Logan motioned to Sophia. "No more, I am leaving"

"And go where?"

"I am going to get the others and set them free of the lords"

"Coriana, you are the eldest tell Logan to stop this" the agitated elder spoke.

All eyes fixed upon her as she thought of her reply. She made her way to the linen closet and took out a sheet and placed it over Sophia's body. She looked up from her crouched position over the young, dead soul and spoke. "Logan has started something that should have begun long before. He has taken the chance where the rest of us were too scared to or too naive, or too contempt."

"Coriana, it is the order" cried the elder.

"It was the order" she removed her self from Sophia, "Today we start anew. All of you go to your chambers and take anything you can carry for we will leave in one hour"

"Where are we going?" Marcus inquired.

"I deemed that we follow Logan's idea. He has obviously thought this through more than any of us had. Go now"

The pack hurried out of the hall save Marcus and Logan. Marcus made his way over Sophia's body. He softly caressed the sheet that laid over his

Chris Crase

beloved. Coriana approached him and offered her condolence of a hand on his shoulder. He looked up and saw her motion him to carry on and prepare for their eminent departure. He regained himself and made his way to his chambers.

Coriana looked to Logan and started to speak, "Logan we have started something here but as you know it will not be easy."

"I know Coriana."

"I just want to know something."

"Anything, but please excuse my nervousness. I am still quite shocked at the events that just transpired."

"I under stand but what I need to know is that are you ready to lead us."

"That is you and the rest of the elders job." Logan answering with a puzzled look.

"It was our way when we knew the way. Logan, being blunt, we the elders are elders because we knew the rules and knew them well and we will not break easy of it as you and the young. We will help Logan, but we need you to step forward and take the steps that you displayed here tonight to see the rest of it through. The young will be easy to persuade to our cause but the old in every castle will not be"

"I understand"

"Good then come and lead us to our new life"

Just after a hour passed when Logan and his pack departed the castle. The moved on ground leaving behind the past. Fearing of the lords, they kept pressing beyond the local towns and made their way past the valleys where none of them had been before. Logan was walking to the side of the pack enjoying the new sights of unseen mountains and streams and trees. That night they slept off the road a couple hundred of yards in a small field of tall grass. Logan had ordered a changing watch to ensure the lords had not trailed them. Logan tried to keep good company but heavy thoughts weighed on him. As the night progressed on the watch changed until Marcus was on duty. Marcus stayed by the fire stoking it partly to keep it going mostly to pass the time. He looked over the pack as they all slept and dreamed. As he gazed through the fire he noticed Logan hunched over on a rock and looking toward the night sky.

He walked over to Logan who kept his gaze upon the stars.

"Cannot sleep Logan?"

"Oh, I guess not I am just thinking"

"It has been a pretty hectic day"

"Yes it has Marcus"

"I never thanked you for helping last night by and by and I wanted to"

"You are welcome, but if you want to thank then listen now"

Never Fall in Love with a Vampire. It is a Pain in the Neck

"Tomorrow I want you to lead some of us north to the castle that lies beyond the two rivers. I need you to go and get the ones that are living there and bring them with us"

"Where are you going?"

"I will a few more toward the west I have heard of another place over there where some of us are working. Coriana will take the rest south as we have been going. In the south there are more lords and more of us the we need to get."

"Why do you want me to go and lead a group to the north. Wouldn't an elder be more appropriate"

"A few elders will go with you but they are still more stuck in the old ways than we are and I think you will have more luck of gaining support from our friends"

"But going north is putting some distance between me and the rest of the pack and is kinda going pack to trouble that we just left"

"Yes, but you are still a ways from Haden and Drake and still the north castle should not be as much trouble as the one in the west."

"Who is at the west?"

"From what I understand the west castle has a very strong contingent of lords. Much worst than Haden and more of them. If Haden is to seek help that is where he would go first so that is why I am taking a group to the west. Get some sleep now you have a long way to go tomorrow. We will discuss with Coriana a meeting place in the morning"

"Are you going to get any sleep?"

"No I will stay up and keep watch."

Thus when morning came, the pack gathered to hear the plan that Logan laid out upon them. Coriana and most of the elders agreed that the most suitable place to meet at was the city that was at the exit of the river that flowed just to the east of the road they were on. Coriana and her group made their way early to cover as much ground as possible during the shortened day. The rest of the pack was split to the best of the ability of the newly endowed leader. Knowing that he needed most of the strong workers, Logan took as many as possible. Marcus was left with most of the younger workers but Logan gave him the two strongest elders that were remaining to help the young novice. The pack said their farewells and made their direction.

Logan pressed on earnestly to get to his fight. He was a good three days travel from the castle and figured that Haden would probably be there awaiting to finish what they had begun. Logan and his contingent wondered through the woods thus no drawing attention to themselves from the villages and travelers. After the arrival of the pack to the castle he made camp to

Chris Crase

wait until the next morning. Logan was planning on maybe a swift departure with his fellow workers from the castle to avoid any conflicts from the lords. Hopefully he imagined a small resistance from the elder workers like his own but the young would more than likely follow suit.

After day break that next morning, Logan led the pack to the castle where he saw the workers emerge from the castle and begin their chores. Logan made his way through the curious, cautious crowd of the on looking workers as the others waited at the gates. The workers of the castle have never met another pack but knew it was a pack nonetheless. Logan approached the elders a greeted them. Logan and the few elders went into the castle to confer. Gradually the two packs began to talk to one another; telling each other of their tales and what has transpired. The workers of the new castle became very interested in Logan's idea and where eager to hear the elders response. Logan's began to urge the workers to prepare to leave so that they could get on the move. Logan and the elders emerge after a hour.

Logan spoke, "This is Friedrich and Aldophus: two of the elders from this castle. They have informed me that the lords were summoned to the castle to the North where Marcus was sent to."

Logan's pack began to get concerned knowing that Logan mistook Haden's plan and went to the weaker castle. Marcus would be surely outmatched with his pack at the northern castle.

Logan continued, "The elders here have agreed to join us and are making preparations to join Coriana in the city. We will go to the northern castle and aid Marcus. Those wishing to join me make ready we leave shortly after sundown."

The lords of this castle had left some of the lower vampire behind to keep order while they convened with Haden and Drake. Logan was eager to see that these vampires did not see another night. Logan disappeared with the elders again to prepare an ambush for nightly rulers. And thus when the sun fell, the vampire lords awoke from their slumber and gathered in the hall.

Logan and the pack waited until all the lords were accounted for and struck down on them. Ripping and tearing the souls from the vampires, the workers made quick work of them. Fifteen dead of the lords laid out across the floor; Logan ordered the workers of the new castle to gather everyone on in the main courtyard. He and his pack stayed behind and gathered the lords up into a gallery of crucifixes as a statement to the high lord of the castle. Logan spared no sympathy on these vampires and as he pierced the dead bodies with wooden stakes he forced the stake stronger and stronger into the next lord. Lastly, Logan set the hall ablaze and walked out to the lead the pack to the north to aid Marcus.

Chapter 20

The northern castle was four days away by walk, but Logan figured as a wolf more ground could be covered. The pack would run a greater risk of being hunted by local villages. Logan pressed on hardly giving the workers anytime to rest for he feared the worst from Haden and Drake for young Marcus. The a couple of workers from the west aided as guides knowing the territory well and the pack easily avoided any problems to the northern castle. They arrived at the fortress in two days, and after pleading with Logan they rested the next. Logan made sure to stay well hidden from the castle that day and night put took a contingent to the castle while the rest of the pack rested during the day.

When they arrived at the castle, he immediately summoned the elder of the workers. Doulph emerged from the stables and greeted Logan and the pack. Very tall and stout in nature was Doulph. Dark thick hair and distinguished eyes set in a stone relief of his face. He naturally walked with the nature of a leader and one could almost feel that as he approached.

"Welcome friends, welcome." Doulph ecstatically pompous.

"Good day friend, I am Logan from the Lord Drake castle and these are the workers from there and from the Lord Aragan castle."

"Ah yes, Marcus said you would come shortly."

"Marcus is here then? Where?"

"Ah, come Logan let us convene and I will tell you what happened."

Logan and Doulph went into the castle as the rest of the pack went about meeting the workers that were busy scrambling about with their daily chores. The workers here were somewhat stand offish with the pack but some of the younger workers did their best to be courteous among stern eyes of the elders.

In the castle the two men sat at the table in the kitchen.

"Logan would you care for a drink?" Doulph offered a chair to him. "Elizabeth would you get our friend a gourd of water."

"So where is Marcus." Logan by passing all pleasantries.

"Marcus and his friends have encountered hard times since you have last seen them."

"What has happened!"

"When Marcus arrived here and found out the lords from your castle came here instead out what you had predicted he figured you would soon be here and decided to play it cautious and camp outside the castle in the woods to the north until you arrived."

"That was smart of young Marcus"

"Yes, he is a bright lad I can see why you put him in charge of the group he led."

"But you said he fell on rough times?"

"Ah, well we tried to keep Marcus a secret from the lords, but one night a lower vampire whom was on a patrol at the request of Lord Haden discovered his camp. The next night, Haden attacked Marcus without any thought of warning. We here at the castle only learned about it the day after. From the reports I have gotten from the eavesdroppers I placed through out the castle at night, Marcus' pack was halved and severely beaten. However, good fortune shined on Marcus and I have heard he escaped with the remaining workers. I have sent out workers during the day to try and locate them and we have found their tracks. Marcus keeps moving around so Haden cannot find him. Fortunately the lords do not have the tracking ability that we possess."

"So you can lead me to Marcus?"

"Ah yes, when we here at the castle heard of what you have done to free us we were more than eager to join you but to save young Marcus we decided to wait for you to give us stronger position. That is why we still carry on our chores."

"That was a wise idea. Now however we are strong. Come let us find my friend Marcus so that he can rejoin the pack and tomorrow we will prepare to take care of Haden."

"I will lead you to your friend Logan. I will also have some of the workers here send supplies to your camp for they must be famished."

"Thank you my friend. Hopefully this will all be done soon and we can join the rest of the pack down the river in the city."

"Come then let us find Marcus before nightfall."

Doulph made arrangements for the workers to take some supplements to Logan's camp and Logan had one of his workers go and show them the way. Doulph found the trackers he had sent out and had them lead Logan, Doulph and the rest of the pack to find Marcus. The trackers led the group in the woods telling Logan that Marcus has been consistently in the thickest of the woods trying to maintain a completely safe atmosphere until he arrived. The forest began to grow thicker and thicker the further along they went. By now it was hard to judge the time of day. The trackers found the camp that Marcus had just abandoned by dusk and told Logan that he should be pretty close by. The trackers went into the wood to try and find the scent of Marcus' pack. Logan had torches made while he waited.

Chapter 21

The ambush started quickly there after. Doulph's pack first emerged with a quick swarm onto Logan and his workers while the vampires came down from the stars. Wasting no time in the confused state, Logan lashed forward with his contingent and rage. Logan and his army used the torches to fend off the pack. Haden struck first at one of workers who was still in a state of bewilderment which fueled Logan to go on the offensive. He immediately transformed into his beast and went after Doulph's pack. He killed five workers within one sweep of the fired clearing. Logan next went after a lord whom was killing his friend. Picking up an extinguished torch on he flight he drove it true with all the anger a man could possess. Logan stood above his dead friend and the vampire and assessed the situation. Even through his valiant effort, his pack was being picked off steadily. He saw Doulph, Haden, and Aragan leading the charge from one end toward him and the rest of his meager pack. Knowing this would be his last stand, he gathered his comrades for one final thrust at the on coming wall of vampires and wolves. Smugness gleamed from the triad that led the army. However, the smugness did not last long as the army was attacked by Marcus from behind. Marcus led his pack with some of the workers from Doulph's pack. The triad quickly turned its attention toward the new front. The once overbearing lords and workers were now spilling blood. With fear of losing the triad ordered the retreat back to castle to refortify their position.

Gathering the rest of them, Logan and Marcus quickly discussed the happenings.

"How are you Marcus?"

"Good, Logan I am sorry for letting this happen."

"What did just happen? We were coming to get you and join the rest of us and the next thing I know Haden and the rest of what seemed the castle attacked us."

"When I got here a couple of days ago, I had not known that Haden and Drake already arrived and were making plans for you. We arrived at dawn to the castle and when we came up to talk with the pack they ambushed us. Drake, Haden, and Lord of this castle, Oman made an agreement with Doulph and some of the workers. We were captured and put in the dungeon to trap you. We were kept under constant scrutiny until tonight that is when I knew that you had come. Luckily some of the workers as you see did not join Doulph and the other lords. They released us and we quickly came to help."

"You should not be ashamed Marcus you did what you had to and thank you for your persistence."

"But alas, as we were being attack Oman and Drake led a group against the others."

"Quickly then, we must return and help them."

They reached the camp just as dawn was creeping over the plains. The camp was nearly destroyed; workers were busy scavenging the remains for friends and supplies. Still others were gathered by glowing embers staying warm against the predawn chill. Logan made his way through the ashes as his comrades went to the aid of their fellows. Broken, shattered, whatever you want to call it described Logan's effort. Not even the pride that he carried of a free man could keep the pain away of the suffering. Always in battle we describe the valiant, never do the stories tell the debt on ones conscience for such nobility. He wandered around looking at the scene in almost disbelief. Overwhelmed by his thoughts, Logan drifted a hundred yards away from the sight and perched himself on a rock next to the river. There he just sat and watched the river flowing in the morning light.

Marcus was busy putting back together the camp and trying to keep hopes alive after the disaster. He worked earnestly through the morning till the camp was ready to leave once again. He looked for Logan and finally found him by the river.

"Logan, he have made ready to move the camp to a safer position and we should get along as quickly as possible."

Logan just sat there motionless staring beyond the river.

"Logan?" Marcus inquiring his response.

"What have I done?" Logan spoke softly.

"How do you mean?"

"Look at what I have done. I have destroyed our friends over my stupid pride."

Marcus feeling where this is going stopped his Logan's pity. "You have done no such thing Logan. You set us free"

"Have I?"

"What were you expecting when you started all this? Did you think it was going to be an easily parade through the country side freeing all of us?"

"I did not know anything that is the problem."

"Quit this nonsense Logan. You have set the ball in motion and now you are frustrated that we hit a hill and we have to do a little pushing, cause I will tell right now that we are willing to push we just need someone to tell us where to push."

Chris Crase

"Where to push huh?" Logan speaking a little sarcastic. "This is where you will push the pack. You will push them down south to the city and join the others."

"What are you talking about?"

"Marcus you will lead our friends away from here. I am going to stay and finish what I have begun with Haden. It is me he wants."

"Then we will stay and help, lest you forget I have a score to finish too."

"Haden does not care about your little dead Sophia"

"I care."

"And what is it that you will do huh? Young Marcus, only a pup, you did not even want to fight I had to coax you into it with my dreams of grandeur."

"I am not going to let you martyr yourself when there is no reason for it."

"You will listen to me and get these workers out of here, lest you forget I m in charge."

Agitated, Marcus response sickened, "Fine I will lead the pack down to the city and we will discuss our next movement, you can go and kill yourself."

Marcus left Logan to stare about the river. Logan stayed for awhile longer with the thoughts in his head and not much else. Eventually he made his way back to the camp. He saw Marcus leading the pack and what was left to the road for exodus. He watched as each one of the workers gave him a blank look passing him. The despair was enough to get to anyone but Logan stood true and without emotion. At last Marcus past him; Logan kept his eyes on his friend as he walked by. Marcus, however, never took his stare off the road in front of him. With each footstep he pierced Logan's heart for the remarks that Logan made upon him. And justly Logan felt them and as the caravan slipped over the last hill a tear rolled down the cheek of Logan.

Chapter 22

Logan made his way to the castle just after the sun hit its apex in the sky. Making his way through the brush he saw the workers carrying on their usual ways. He slipped to the nearest point of coverage at the opened main gate and waited until a trailer to return. And as one of the trailers made its way into the castle he rolled with it into the courtyard. There he made his way around hay bails and stables. He overheard some of the workers talking with sympathy about the tragedy and how they wished they could have done something. Others gossiped that were sent to eye the camp. They informed Doulph that the camp had retreated. Doulph grinned at the news and informed his friends that they would seek them out as soon as the lords awoke. Doulph then proceeded into a far door and into the castle to make preparations for the night's attack.

Logan awaited for his chance to slip into the castle door without attention and soon got his wish. He made his way down the corridor following the scent of Doulph. He soon caught up with Doulph whom was sitting at a table in a small room at the back of the kitchen. Logan entered the room and Doulph looked up at him across the table.

"Good show Logan. I had a feeling I would be seeing you."

"Why did you do it?"

"Why? Why does a man do anything in this world Logan? Power."

"You sold us out."

"I sold you out, but as for me and the rest we are doing just fine."

"What did Haden promise you."

"Haden gave me control over the workers. I am what you call a duke or something on that order to the peons that I once was myself."

"You were a duke but now you are a dead monarch."

"Oh come Logan. I thought more of you than a person who makes idle threats"

"You are right."

Logan turned the table over that separated the two and attacked Doulph. Doulph was quick to react and transformed into himself and threw Logan into the corner.

Looking down upon Logan, Doulph said, "Now what are you planning to do? die a martyr?"

"No, just to die and take as many of you with."

Logan lunged as he became his beast and pushed Doulph against the wall. Each wolf struggle for position against one another. Resisting every motion the other made until Logan tripped up Doulph on the table. With

Chris Crase

every ounce of himself, Logan killed Doulph. He tore and bit the beast underneath him. Logan then found his mark and gripped his teeth around the throat of Doulph. Doulph tried to push away from Logan but alas his hand fell limp as the last breath of Doulph's tainted life left him. Logan filled with adrenaline and vengeance did not release his grip on Doulph and he kept tearing the dead animal beneath him.

It was not until three workers pulled Logan off and restrained him that he let go of Doulph. The workers quickly dragged Logan to a room and locked him in until nightfall. Hours passed as Logan calmly sat in his room. He opted for his beast form rather than his worker. He, in his gray and black fur, quietly hunched over with his hands over his face. The sun began to move down and rays of light explicitly wandered through his small window. His fur jacket lighted up with blood soaked soft tones. Pondering his known last sunset Logan began to stand up to reach the star. Looking up at the sky in a broken down stance he felt a wound on his leg. Logan looked down to examine the wound. He looked at the leg and then started to look over his wolf body. The light striking his body lighted it up like the bush of fire. And as he looked over his body he realized that he never was his wolf, he hid it from himself almost ashamed of it. So as the sun showered him he looked back at it with a sharp tooth grin and howled out in the glory of what he is.

Logan's howl rang over the courtyard and pierced the sounds of the workers in the castle. They all stopped their work to listen to the rejoicing howl from the small prison room, pondering its mad meaning. And over the hillside the true animal called wolf and the wild dogs about joined in on the last song. The howls echoed within every crack of the countryside and castle.

Chapter 23

Twilight came and howls stopped as the lords came out. Haden requested a congregation of the castle in the great hall to witness the demonstration he intended for Logan. And thus the workers gathered in the hall at the respectful end and waited as the lords made there way one by one in their own time. Haden made his way in last with Drake, Oman, and Aragan. They walked through the workers and the other lords to their places at the other end of the hall upon some makeshift stages. Haden stepped forward and silence fell over the crowded room. Aragan motioned to some of the lords who responded by taking a few workers with them out of the hall to retrieve Logan from his prison. As the group was gone, Drake motioned to another group of workers whom quickly erected a magnanimous X from logs in the middle of the hall. The fire fell light upon the X causing a shadow to cover the workers. Just as the workers were finishing tying down the structure, the group of lords emerge with the workers holding Logan. Logan made no attempt to resist the stronghold of his own. The eyes of the hall caste themselves onto Logan as they led him to the X. Haden and Oman were engaged in small talk with grinning triumph on their faces. Logan fixed his eyes upon their faces as he was escorted to his death. Haden and Oman broke their verse and glared back. Neither side gave a sign of perpetual weakness. The workers tied Logan to the X as the lords and their fellow packed looked on. After the workers finished the preparations, everyone returned to their place in the hall. Haden stepped forward after what could have been deemed an eternity.

He spoke. "Magnificent Logan, where is your magnificence now? Where is your pack? Where is your spirit? What have you done?"

Addressing the hall, Haden continued louder. "I will answer these questions for our silent guest. Your magnificence was a fantasy, your pack has long since retreated in defeat, your spirit is mine and you have done nothing… Look around broken soul, life continues on just as it has. The workers are still working the lords are still the masters of the night and their castles. Oh, you might think to yourself that at least your pack has made it out. But where will they go? What will they do? You have thrown them out into the cruel world. They shall be hunted down, but not by us but by the people you strive so hard to be. They will hunt down your friends and kill them to feed their hatred. What have you done poor Logan, you have sent your friends to death. At least we the lords protected you and your pack from that world and yourselves."

Haden turned around from Logan to address the rest of the masses.

Chris Crase

"We cannot allow this worker to continue on. He must die to protect us and our way. He must die in this way to serve as an example to the rest of us, so that we may learn not to be misguided in our thoughts. This is the way and it will remain the way. Who is he to upset our balance?"

Turning back to Logan. "Good bye my good, mislead worker."

Haden solemnly made his way back to his position with Oman. He whispered something to Oman onto which Oman nodded in approval. Then Haden motioned to the lower vampires whereupon they rushed to Logan and began to feast upon him. Eight of them were scraping over the X to get a nice piece of Logan and the rest surrounded the X to protect the others. Like a pack of rats they scurried over their victim as Logan tried not to let out his pain.

Minutes passed as the orgy of death continued. Haden finally spoke to Oman who made his way down to stopped the vampires. They pulled away, reluctantly, from Logan but still obeying their lord. Logan was draped in blood and nearly unconscious. His body lay limp upon his X as the blood poured down onto the ground. With the vampires pulled back around Logan, Haden then waved Drake forward.

Haden spoke, "Lord Drake has suffered the most at the hands of this worker. For you see my congregation his wife was taken by Logan. Thus I give Drake the right to end this worker's life."

And so Haden stepped out of the way of Drake and ushered him by with his hands to Logan. Drake stepped of the stage and proceeded to Logan. He stopped in front of wolf and lifted Logan's chin and gazed into his eyes with his own satisfaction. Looking at Logan's exhausted face, Drake's satisfaction turned to anger. He dropped Logan's chin and stepped back and backhanded the dead face. Drake proceeded to the fireplace and took up the stoker and made his way back through the workers and the vampires.

"Wait!" Haden sternly spoke up. Everyone turned to Haden for his announcement except Drake whose anger he wanted to keep focused.

Haden continued, "I must asked the workers to kneel in respect of your lords before Lord Drake ends this dissidents life. It is the only the right thing to do. Please workers, kneel down and accept your allegiance to us lords. Do this out of respect for us and yourselves and for our suffering friend Lord Drake."

And by and by the workers fell down to their knees, as the Lord Haden requested. As the last of the workers fell down in the back of the hall, Drake pulled the stoker above his head to bury into the soul of Logan. Then was when the hall noticed the one worker dressed in a hooded gown with his face hidden. The shadow of the X fell onto his body and the shrouded worker stood above the rest. He quietly made his way through the knelt

Never Fall in Love with a Vampire. It is a Pain in the Neck

bodies surrounding him and into the opening behind the X. Everyone watched as he transcended the hall and moved around the X. He stopped in front of Logan facing Drake and the lords behind him.

Marcus removed his hood to face the vampires with a defiance upon his body and soul. With a look of disbelief on the congregation, Marcus became with his animal form and with an awesome look upon his wolf eyes he spoke.

"I am here to finish what my friend Logan started."

And with that he rushed at Haden. From the wall came the rest of the exodus pack, attacking every lord and any worker that defended them. The blitzkrieg of the assault handed Marcus several deaths of the lower vampires. On the stage, Haden, Oman, and Aragan banded with other vampires to hold off the workers. Marcus was fighting through the vampires protecting the stage and as Marcus rose onto the platform and face Haden and the others, Haden yelled out to Drake.

"Kill him!!"

Drake turned around and threw the stoker into Logan. Logan yelled out a howl and then fell dead as Drake turned around to face the fight. Drake was met by a three of Logan's and Marcus' friends whom quickly pounced him and took him to the depths of his hatred. Drake's tormented cries did not last long as the wolves ripped his being to shreds.

Meanwhile, Marcus stood confronted on the stage with the lords many of whom were fighting off Marcus' allies. Oman engaged Marcus first as Haden floated to higher ground to oversee the destruction. More and more of workers were turning on him and fighting with Marcus. Marcus took Oman to the ground with an attitude of superior cause. As he clawed the life out of the weaker Oman, lower vampires desperately tried to attack Marcus whose hidden strength came out as he threw them back while he finished Oman. With Oman all but alive, Marcus took his ground again staring down the lower vampires as they frantically withdrew to find an easier battle. Aragan was still left on the stage dealing with ease yet another of the workers, killing three himself.

Aragan threw off his latest victim and turned to face Marcus, for they deserved each other in battle. So from either end of the stage of bodies, blood, and fighting they flung themselves at each other. Their battle pushed everyone off the stage as the workers were causing the vampires to retreat hastily to Haden's position. All looked upon the two warriors on the stage as neither was giving way in their war.

Haden, realizing his lost, ordered the vampires to retreat into the night air as he himself slowly retreated looking onto his lord starting to lose to Marcus' strength. Fore for every time Aragan inflicted a wound upon

Chris Crase

Marcus, he would instantly recover and come back to Aragan twice fold. Finally the weakness took its toll on Aragan and his lost his footing and fell to the ground. Marcus, not hesitating, fell onto the lord with his paws and teeth. Haden turned to flee when he saw his warrior had lost.

Thus was the end. In a few years the workers from all over disbanded from their old life with relative ease. They left mostly during the day when the lords could do nothing. Now and then there was an incident with one decisive victor whether it be the lords or the workers. But in the end the workers had left and retreated to secluded parts around the world to live their own lives in their packs. Marcus and his pack lived for awhile in the city at the foot of the river mixing in with the cosmopolitans, but eventually left to the new world and opted for a secluded life. Every now and then a member left to venture out into the world. The lords formed the council headed by Haden to oversee their new life and to keep the rest of the vampires as strong as they could.

Never Fall in Love with a Vampire. It is a Pain in the Neck

Chapter 24

It was around a week before Christine was able to escape the ever growing presence of vampires. Morgan did his best to throw off the questions of the clan that increasingly pressed. So after a week when the bulk of the vampires had assembled and their questions where dulling down, Christine assumed her normal role of seducing and killing young men.

She woke that night and put on one of her vixen dresses and informed Morgan that she was leaving him and the others to fend for themselves, as she was tired of playing tour guide. Morgan himself had grown tired of the nightly gatherings, thus he agreed with Christine.

About a hour after leaving her apartment, Christine called Leif. She got his answering machine. Frustrated, Christine left a message to meet her at Charlie's bar on the beach. She then took painstaking effort to elude anyone of her vampire friends which could have trailed her. Especially since the twins have grown suspicious of her actions over the last week.

Christine thus drove her car down to a parking lot of a strip mall. The corner of the parking lot was dark whereupon an easily avoidable spot for women; the strip mall had a club in it called The City. A month before it was known as The Palace, two months before, Retro, on month before, Hot Times, three months before, Beaches. The City as it is called now is the typical strip mall club. It's name changes every time the bouncer lets in the 14 year old who gets drunk thus impregnated by the 26 year old who is dressed to impress no one but the 14 year olds so when the mother finds out the club is sued or fines and what not and then has to shut down to the next owner or same come in and do it again. Anyhow, Christine proceeds stealthily from her car to the club whereupon the bouncer tells her of the club policy to check for concealed weapons. Probably the reason it shut down last time. The bouncer pats her down sparing no space for her to hide a tattoo let alone a gun or a knife. He then asks her for her ID whereupon he states $10 dollars under, $5 dollars over.

Christine thinks to herself, "I cannot think of why this place always shuts down and reopens all the time."

Christine pays the cover and enters the packed club. She made a round of the club to see if anyone of her friends had followed her. She thought she noticed one of the twins, but alas it was not him. Feeling pretty confident, she waited for a group of drunkards to leave and she snuck out of the club with them.

Chris Crase

Leaving her car there as a precautionary, Christine took a cab from the club to Charlie's. She was running late and she had hoped that she did not miss Leif.

She entered Charlie's and sat down at the bar. Charlie was in the back helping the cook. When he emerged form the kitchen, tying his apron, he took one look up at his new customer, "Ah, Christine, how are ya eh?"

"Good Charlie, how are you?"

"You know, my little wife, she justa bugs the hell outta me. Ya know saying I'a spend to much time here and drinking. Then I'sa go home and she yells at me some more." Laughing.

"Maybe you should not drink anymore Charlie."

"Maybe I shouldn't go home a no more!"

"That could work too." Both laughing.

Charlie returns with a beer for Christine and says, "I know you are looking for the Leifer, but I hadn't seen him in here yet."

"Thanks Charlie, I will just wait around for him."

"Ya wanna eat something?"

"No thank you."

"Wella just help ya self to the beer. I am gonna be taking care of the other customers." Charlie scampers off into the kitchen to help the cook once more.

Christine lights up a cigarette and looks over the bar. The restaurant was surprisingly busy for the night; there was a lot of out of town families mixing with the locals. When Charlie had a minute, Christine inquired about the volume of the restaurant. It turned out that there was a town festival happening for the small suburb. Christine noticed one family sitting close to her. They were a middle age family that all looked like they were in the most excruciating pain of their lives. A family get together, organized by the mom, enforced by the father who would rather be riding a lawn mower than worry about his teenage daughter getting knocked up. The son who cares more at that age of trying to knock up his father's best friends daughter and whether or not his effort in the off season in the gym has caught Christine's attention. The daughter who is worried about her mom finding out about her abortion. The mom worried if everyone is having a good time. A typical American family.

Christine remembers her own family. Her mother was taken ill and died after her little brother's birth. Her brother died shortly after. All she remembers of him was his big blue eyes, just like her fathers. After the death of her mother and brother, Christine's dad tried to raise Christine. Having problems with that, Christine ran away after ten years of fighting his authority. That was the last time she saw him alive. He died of old age.

Never Fall in Love with a Vampire. It is a Pain in the Neck

Lighting another cigarette, Christine thinks of the time when her father tried to cook her dinner for her birthday. He was awfully inept in the kitchen not to mention the rest of the home. Her father desperately made her favorite food at the time and almost ended up hacking off all his fingers, burning down their home, and giving them both gas poisoning. After all that the main course was still quite good, even with the blackened bread served with it.

Turning back to reality for a spell, Christine helps herself to another beer as Charlie ran amuck. Christine glances at the time and notices that a hour has almost past. She begins to think that Leif might not show up. She decides that it is still rather early and she did kinda assumed he would be around. She put her beer down and went to the restroom. After emerging from the restroom, that she had been in forever. I can't really explain what happens in there cause I am a male. Christine makes her way over to the jukebox and threw on some top forty tunes to lighten up her and the bored families. She returned to her drink and waited for Leif.

After about another hour and two more drinks, Leif came scampering into the bar. I came in huffing and puffing; I bend over to catch my breath and look up to Chris giggling at me. So I stood up, still out of breath, and puffed out my chest as I tried to take small breaths as I walked over to join her. I calmly wave to Charlie along the way.

"Man, I gotta quit smoking!" lighting up a cig.

"Somehow I do not think smoking would affect you that much Leif." smiling.

"Yeah, you are probably right, weird though eh?"

"What did you do? Hear my message and run all the over here?"

"Well actually the truth of it is that I was home when you called but I let my answering machine get it cause I have this psycho wench stalking for the past week."

"Really!?" sarcastically.

"Yep, anyway I went down to catch the bus over here right after you called but the strangest thing then happened. I was on the bus when this group of hippies got on board and tried to hijack it."

"No, you are joking."

"It gets even weirder. Well we started to head off to Frisco cause that is where the hippies wanted to go but along the way this alien ship came down upon us."

"I suppose they then took you captive?"

"No, that would be absurd. But because of their highly advanced propulsion system, the bus stopped working. The hijackers, however, were so scared that they split so me and a few other riders of the public

Chris Crase

transportation system had to push the bus to a gas station. That is why I am out of breath."

"Oh, makes sense to me. I am just glad the hippies did not hurt you."

"Hold on a sec while I grab a beer." Leif proceeds to jump the counter and land directly on his stomach on the other end. Christine looks over as she hears Leif mumbling about having to try and be cool. Leif gets up and clears his throat as he dusts himself off. I proceed to fill a mug and walk around the bar to rejoin Chris.

"How have you been, Chris?"

"Pretty good considering all the hoopla I have been going through. And yourself?"

"I am all right. I have been hanging around my old friends catching up on the ties. Say that family over there looks like they are having a terrible dinner." As I motion to the family over Christine's shoulder.

"Yeah, they look pretty sad."

"So have ya missed me, huh, huh?" prodding Chris.

"Not really, I have seeing some men at night so I haven't really had time to think of you."

"Really? Are they nice men?"

"Oh yes, this one named Jim is just dazzling. He is sharp looker and very successful. He is an accountant."

"Sounds like a winner but can he jump over a bar?"

"Nah, he made the waitress do it." Christine smiles.

"Well, then... I am at a loss for words." I replaced my lean with the barstool and lit up another cigarette. "So are your friends pretty pissed a me?"

"I don't think pissed is the right word for it. I mean at first they were but when they found out you where a well you know, they became the anger of which God has in the bible."

"Oh well I guess that little incident a few years ago is still burning them."

"Yep, they haven't got over that yet."

"No doubt, a bunch of my friends are still ticked off too."

"How many of your friends are here?"

"Couple hundred, you?"

"About the same, the council I guess is arriving sometime and that entourage will be around fifty or more."

"The council?"

"We set up a council after that past thing where about twenty of the eldest and most powerful lords reside."

"So you guys are a hierarchy."

"Not so much anymore, but they do govern us and make sure things like this are swiftly taken care of without much noise."

"The Mafia then."

"Ha, yeah I guess we could be like that."

"They are coming then eh. I imagine Haden will be along with them."

"Pretty much count on it. I have never met the council and they do want to meet with me upon their arrival."

"Check you out. Miss Popular now."

"Yeah, I just wish it was under circumstances."

"Tell me about it I guess Marcus is coming down and I have to met with him too."

"What are you going to tell him and your friends."

"The truth."

"The truth?"

"Yep, I am going to tell them that I met this insufferable bitch that I happened to fall in love with and by the way she is a vampire and I killed one of her friends who just happened to be one too."

Grinning Chris leans into me. "So who is this other vampire slut in this town that you fell in love with cause I am gonna kick her ass."

"Oh there is no one else I was referring to you as the insufferable bitch."

"I might be a bitch but I think I am tolerable." Smiling.

"You see there you go again cracking that smiling and looking at me with those big eyes, insufferable!"

"You know it."

After sitting at Charlie's till closing time, we bided Charlie adieu. We strode along the beach with the few hours that Christine had left. We just goofed around while the surf covered our toes and the crescent moon covered the ocean. As the night carried on I learned that Chris has been a long time traveler of the world. Spending most of her time in the old country. She was telling me stories about the Spanish empire and how she did meet Christopher Columbus once when he was a teenager. And she starting speaking all these languages more than I ever knew but we did have some fun talking Latin while we put on a little impromptu play. Then she kissed me good night and was gone. I made my way back to my pad whereupon I showered the sand, seawater, beer, and smoke off my body and retired to my bed.

Chris Crase

Chapter 25

The next morning I woke up with the doc making a loud ruckus in my kitchen. I walked out of my bedroom to be blasted by fresh air and sunlight. Taking two steps back I let out a shriek of disappointment that even the wicked witch of the east would have been impressed.

"Morning sunshine!" The Prof grinned.

"Ah shit Doc, how did you get in here?"

"I asked the land lady to let me in. You would be surprised at what being a clean cut person can get you."

"Don't remind me, maybe some day I will shape up."

"Where the heck do you keep the coffee filters?"

"Over there," I pointed.

"Ah, do like your coffee strong?"

"Not too strong." I sat down and lit a smoke.

The Prof finished brewing the coffee and washing out two cups and brought over one.

"Beautiful day today isn't it Leif."

"First of all it is not day yet it is the morning and it is too bright."

"Boy, someone sure gets cranky before his first cup of coffee."

"I ain't cranky I am just having caffeine withdrawals." I grinned as I proceed to slurp my coffee. "So what is new with you I haven't seen you in a couple of days."

"Oh, nothing I have just been helping out the local kids clubs and stuff. I also have a few young adults that moved down here that I helped awhile ago so I visited them."

"What are they up to?"

"One is studying engineering at the college and the other is a director of youth activities at a elementary school." The Prof knows I am always willing to help him.

"Well tell the guy who is in engineering if he needs help I am available."

"Maybe I will but the shape you are in. There is no way you could help out the others."

"Hey its the life of a med student" I smirk.

"Anyway," the doc sitting down in a chair, "How was your date last night."

"How did you know? Did you follow me?" I was getting a little ticked off.

Never Fall in Love with a Vampire. It is a Pain in the Neck

"Relax Leif, let me explain. I was on my way over here last night to see if you wanted to get a cup of coffee and discuss a novel that I know you have read and to tell you something else." I saw you head out of your apartment in a hurry. I figure you were going to see Christine, that is her name isn't it? I sorry but curiosity killed the cat so yeah I did follow you. She seems nice enough I would have never guessed she was a vampire. Great smile too."

"Hey, she is a bit young for you, don't you think."

"I don't know how old is she."

Stumped I scratched my head, "Ya know, I have no idea."

We both kinda chuckled about that notion for a couple of seconds.

"So Prof, what was the novel."

"Oh yeah it is called The First Nine."

"Good book, crappy ending but all in all a good book."

"Yep, that is pretty much what I thought."

"So what was this something you had to talk to me about."

Breaking his thought on the book he takes a drag from his smoke.

"Marcus is here," The Prof stands up and reaches in his pocket, "He wants to see you this afternoon. Here is his address."

Looking at the piece of paper, "Is this a group intervention or."

"Oh, no I hardly explained the whole situation to him, I left that to you so it is just you two."

"Much obliged"

"By and by, Timmy is in town finally. I arranged for you, me, him, Scotty, and Jimmy to go out tonight. He will picked you up around nine."

"Cool, hopefully Marcus will leave a bit of my ass unchewed so I can make it."

"Keep your chin up kid" The Prof starts to gather his things. "Until tonight young squire. Adieu."

"Later Doc."

The Doc closed the door and I heard his footsteps going down the stairs. I lit up another smoke and fell back onto the couch. Looking at the address I put my arm over my eyes and mumble, "Man I hate Mondays, nothing has ever come out of a Monday that is good."

Chapter 26

I got dressed and headed out to meet with Marcus. His address was in the mud hills of L.A. so I took my time to get there. I went around the campus first trying to get in contact with my teachers to tell them I was not going to be around for a few days. I bullshitted with some and left notes at the others along with some thoughts on their upcoming lectures. I stopped by the computer cluster to read my e-mail and surf the net. I then proceeded down to the coffee shop and relaxed for a couple of hours. There was a couple of my class mates at the coffee place so I sat with them and they asked me a tonne of questions about the classes. Even though I was slacking off this semester I still seemed like the man with the answers. I hate that. People tapping your brain and you being nice give them the answers and then when you mess up one time they never let you forget it. I guess it makes them feel better, but then again I don't mess up, usually.

After a while I became bored repeating medical anatomy so I proceeded to change the subject to philosophy. They all seemed pretty interested and only a few could engaged me in the conversation. I even learned a little bit. blah blah blah blah.

Anyway after I left the scene of my cohorts into the rest of my day I went down to the convenient store and grab a couple packs of smokes and perused the magazine rack of fleshy women just for kicks. The day was warming up as I made my way back through campus and started a more direct path to the residence of Marcus as I was running late. Up through the hills, I followed somewhat familiar hills and turns until I arrived at the house. I knocked at the door and was greeted by a young attractive women which caught me by surprise. I stumbled back and looked at the crumbled the note with the address and checked the numbers on the wall. Confused I asked her if this was the correct house. But before I finished the question she spoke.

"You must be Leif" with a smile.

"Ah, yep."

"Marcus is waiting for you by the solarium with his tea."

"Oh, thank you as I entered the big big house."

"Come on I will show you."

As she led me down the stairs I asked her her name.

"Cloe" she stated without an offbeat step in her movement as if she was thinking "man what a dork".

I entered the solarium that had already missed the sun's morning presence and it seemed to remind me of a cloudy New York day. I saw a

Never Fall in Love with a Vampire. It is a Pain in the Neck

man sitting at one of those cheap wooden round table facing me with tea set in front of him. Marcus got up and approached me with a friendly face. A very intimidating person Marcus was. The type of person who has been through the shit of the shit and now is carefree. One would almost mistake it for crazy but he was just one of those men. I had to go the bathroom.

"Leif, I must admit your friends do not do a very good job of describing you."

"And onto you as well Marcus," as we shook hands.

"Please sit, a cup of earl gray?"

"Sure thank you."

"I do not think Cloe will mine if you smoke in here." as he eyed her to retrieve the necessary amenities to comfort me. Marcus regained his chair and took up his tea as he laid back studying me.

"Pretty nice accommodations here Marcus, especially the maid. Yuk, yuk" I grinned at him.

"Cloe is actually the owner of this place and she has graciously allowed me to stay here for this ordeal."

"Oh, how do you know her."

"I met her a couple centuries ago. She was the first one I knew that was a North American by right."

"Really, I figured I was the only one in LA."

"And insomuch as that goes I have had her watching you for a while."

"Pard me" I was both got off guard and interested in his statement that I could not express the anger which should be incorporated with such an action.

"Oh, don't get me wrong it started before you met Christine, I have long heard about you Leif and usually like to keep tabs on your next crusade."

"Huh, why do you find me so interesting?"

"Well I think it is because first of all you are interesting, even before you met Tim and changed your life. You have always shot for the stars and now with what we have given you a.k.a. immortality you are abusing the hell out it. You want to do everything and you are wasting no time."

"I just like to see what I cannot do."

"Have you found anything you cannot do?"

"Keep out of trouble."

"Ha, yes I have to agree with that otherwise I would not be here."

"So what has Cloe told you about me."

"What I got from her is that you seem not to have a care in the world just walking around doing what ever you want becoming what you will but then again it is more like you care about other things that regular Joes do not. It like you care about the real stuff which makes you more

Chris Crase

unapproachable because people see that about you and don't know what it is all about."

"You got that all from what she has described of me."

"Yes it is very interesting and I guess I have already knew that about you and that is why I keep tabs on you."

"I feel quite embarrassed at all these compliments, I thought I was boring individual trying to obtain some sort of hero status."

"She also said that you become unbelievably happy when you meet up with Chris. It is as if you take one more step above the rest of us into a abyss of joy around her."

"And I guess that is the problem isn't it."

"Tell me about her."

"She feeds my soul. I mean I feel like when I am with her, the world which I have seen and been apart of in all its wonderful misery disappears and she reminds me of the good that the world could be and that I can help it become."

"Shit, I was just expecting the 'I love her' speech. I guess we do have a problem then don't we Leif."

"I would like to think that it was just hers and mine but if the problem is not resolved here and now it only be cropped up again, we cannot keep brushing this shit under the rug you know."

"I know, I know. So if I am be convinced you have to tell me more about this lord which you have been smitten over."

Never Fall in Love with a Vampire. It is a Pain in the Neck

Chapter 27

Have you ever come across someone where you swear that you must have done something to appease the gods to have them introduce you to this person. Ah, but though it may seem as if it were a gift of gold it was only the wrapping. And then you have realized that you have to aspire to receive that once perceived gift. Thus you have to pull out all your tricks and trade secrets to woo this one, only then to have to throw all that away and reveal yourself: stripped down to the under belly of your soul. Some, most do not make it claiming fool's gold or worse the ability not to undo the tricks and treats. Great tragedies on both aspects: on one end you can trick yourself into closing your mind and making the person ashamed of themselves and on the other end you close your mind and make yourself look pathetic.

But if you can tolerate the madness you create for this person in your heart and mind. If you can push threw the fear, trust; if you can push towards what is the unknown, the mystery; if you have the endurance and faith to push. You can then bear all unknowing and proudless, then my friend you begin to learn. The person, themselves, begin to process of resurrection too. Finding once to be only the dreams of the poets, the understanding that only geniuses possess. And to what is found can only be short of heaven or hell itself, nothing in this world can touch the truth that exists between the two. That is the true gift: the process of falling in love and not love itself. It is a scary truth that exists unknowing and for the most part unwanting. And with that gift you never lose, you will be in a violent, enduring, miraculous free fall.

The rest shall fear you and loathe you claiming you two, one as charlatans. Consummating the sanctified bond of tricks and treats till death due them apart, they shall scowl and hunt you without success. At every turn they will try to undo the one, two. Life cannot be forgiving to this for it can be the very essence of life that everyone can feel and dread. It is the hate in us past down though the bloodlines from one generation to the next. For having something they cannot understand and fear, the rest shall die in comfort of knowing they resisted it, resisted in all their faculties; yours will be the one without death. Thus is the gift, thus is the hope, and thus... what I have. Fuck'em all.

Chapter 28

When it was time for Christine to convene with the council, it was an interesting adventure. She woke that night to the sound of Morgan knocking on her door with the twins. Morgan informed her that it was the night upon which the council wishes to bring her forth to hear her testimony. Christine was to appear before all that had come to L.A.

After Morgan had explained to her the night activities, Christine slowly made herself available to travel with him to the meeting grounds. She threw herself together in about a hour while the guys hung around her living room. Ever being thorough the twins kept pressing her to hurry and Morgan just sat there reading a history book, Christine was able to bring herself together and join the men in the living room. At this time the twins had helped themselves to the wine in her makeshift apartment bar and Morgan was on the balcony smoking a cig.

Christine made handy a glass of wine for herself and joined Morgan on the balcony.

"Can I have one of your cigarettes?" She asked Morgan.

Morgan reached into his pocket and grabs his lighter and smokes, "Here you go", handing the items to Christine.

She lights up a smoke and sips some wine as she turns her back to the living room and Morgan to stare out into the city's night. Morgan continues to eye the twins in the living room.

"Have you seen him?" he inquires.

"It has been a couple of days."

"How is holding up?"

"Oh, I do not know, he really does not let anything show. Leif almost exists outside the world you know."

"Sounds a little weird to me."

"Nah, just eccentric." she smiles at L.A. as if remembering something about Leif that she enjoyed.

"Humpf, well anyway Christine tonight might be a little rough. You are going to have every eye on you while the council talks to you about this Leif guy. And Lord Haden will be very inquisitive so watch yourself. Haden seems to be quite taken with you from what he has heard so that is another thing to watch out for tonight."

"Anything else I should know about this night or in that matter any other night since or to come?"

"Just be strong like you are, do not falter and be intimidated by the council. They are pretty rough as I was saying but knowing you..." Morgan grins through the glass at the twins and continues, "The lords should be worried more about you."

"Well then..." Christine finishes her wine and takes a drag from the cig and flicks it unto the street below, "lets get this done with."

Christine, Morgan, and the twins left her apartment and made their way to her car. The twins hopped in the back and Morgan proceeded into the passenger seat. Christine started her car, gave it a few good throttles and was off in the direction that Morgan told her. The twins desperately fumbled to get their seatbelts on as Christine made it an effort to have them tossed around for awhile while their hands where under the seat looking for the straps. Driving through highways and byways, alleyways and parkways, Christine and her trio found themselves in the center of Beverly Hills approaching a hotel. Christine pulled into the driveway as the twins hopped out before the valet got to the car.

Morgan patiently waited as Christine checked her lipstick in the rearview mirror. Morgan then got out at the assistance of the valet and stood there waiting for Christine. Morgan had the stance of looking the fool for the twins lack of courtesy of which usually occurs when a child among their parents and parents friends does something like scratching the car of their friends. The parents obviously ashamed at the accident that they almost alienate the child by convincing themselves that it was not little Billy that did it.

So as Christine and Morgan proceeded to the lobby of the hotel at least eight steps ahead of the twins. The twins looked at each other with dumfounded expressions of what did we do now. Upon entering the hotel the magistrate came out from nook or shadow to inquire about their needs.

"Are you here for the banquet tonight sir?" he bothered Morgan.

"Yes we are."

"Please follow me." as the magistrate stepped down the long lobby.

Christine entered a great room with round dining tables filled by vampires from all walks of life. The conversation amongst the lords died quickly and was replaced by gazing eyes and whispers. The magistrate led Christine and Morgan to the front of the room to a table with some of the council at it. The twins took seats in the back with some of their closer friends. Christine sat next to Morgan at one of the three tables reserved for the council, her, and him. Upon ordering wine from the waiter, Christine noticed an empty seat around the table. Becoming somewhat nervous she lit a cigarette and began to converse with Morgan as the stares stopped and the conversations resumed.

Christine kept up her conversation with Morgan while eyeing the empty chair. Morgan was busy telling her of the council members at their table.

Chris Crase

Every now and then an old friend of Morgan's would come by and say hello as an excuse to measure up Christine to the other lords.

As the meals began to come out, Christine began to relax about the empty chair. She assured herself that it was a goof up by the hotel about the numbers. She took a deep breath of relief and began to eat her dinner. She started a conversation with one of the council members to her side. It was a pretty good meal: sautéed beef strips in a marinade, rare, served on a bed of pasta with an acute garlic sauce. As good as the meal was, it was twice as big. About midway through the course, Christine was about to call it quits when one of the council members looking through her shouted.

"Haden where have you been?"

Christine felt the presence of a person making their way from the walkway behind her around the table. Haden spoke.

"My dear apologies my friends, I was held up by my servant who seem to have misplaced my pants and tie."

Haden is now standing behind his chair. Wearing an all black suit with no tie, his hands were resting on the back of the chair. He looked as if he was one of the most successful and youngest looking bankers in the history of the world. His distinguished features and broad shoulder complimented his stone cut face and graying sideburns.

"I finally had to settle for this old suit!" Haden said smiling.

"Ah," a council member breaks in, "you probably made your servant Achilles run out and buy you that suit and then made him stay in your room until he found your clothes."

"You know me too well my old friend" Haden laughed acknowledging that familiar faces at the table. "However I do not know these two lords that are gracing our presence."

Morgan stood up and announced him and Christine to Haden. Christine slowly made her way out of the chair as she saw Haden making his way to them.

"Ah, yes Morgan, I think I do remember meeting you once before. Years ago perhaps during the inquisition I believe. Never get old Morgan," Haden taping the side of his head with a smirk, "You start to lose your mind."

That remark eased Morgan's tension of the moment and chuckled as he shook Haden's hand.

"And you Christine have created quite a stir in our community."

"Yes, I suppose I have haven't I?"

"Not to worry young angel we are here to help you out of it."

"Yes my lord." releasing her hand from his.

Never Fall in Love with a Vampire. It is a Pain in the Neck

"Well, I suppose I have some catching up to do, don't I?" as Haden proceeded back to his chair and sat down. A waiter quickly brought him the dish. Christine, wanting to avoid socializing with the all too willing Haden, made herself hungry again and ate the rest of the dinner slowly but always with food in the mouth.

Haden was his usual affable self, catering to the conversations among the table. Jumping into a thought here and a joke there, he commanded the socialization. And thus after the cheesecake: New York, Haden was the first to break the uncomfortable situation that arose: the point of the dinner.

Standing up he placed his hands upon the table and gave a once quick over, "Well, we should begin considering the night will not be young forever and some of us lords have other business to attend to."

And with that, the council made their way upon the stage behind the tables prepared like a trial. Christine lit a cigarette. Some of the lords issued the wait staff out and closed the doors behind them. Next the lords dimmed the lights and place more candles at the councils staged table and Christine and Morgan's table to assure the focal points of the meeting. Haden's servant then appeared and was rushing about with a carafe of wine filling all the council member's glasses. Haden motioned to him to scurry over to him. Haden spoke softly into his ear and pointed to Christine and Morgan. The servant with that hopped down from the stage and made his way to the table with his carafe.

"Wine?" he inquired with a soft childlike voice.

Morgan nodded and the servant filled his goblet. After filling Morgan's glass, the servant of Haden proceeded to begin to fill Christine's when she abruptly stopped him.

"Actually I would like a beer, not a light beer, nor cheap, but not an import either." she spoke persistently.

The server was taken aback and gave a flustered look to Morgan. Morgan bit his lip and lowered his head hoping not to bear a grin. The servant getting no help from Morgan looked over his shoulder at Haden praying that his master could resolve the uneasiness he orchestrated.

Catching his servant in a glance while discussing with a councilmen, Haden inquired, "What is the problem?"

"She wants a beer." he looked as if he was going to break into tears.

"Well go to the wait staff and see if they can get her one." Haden spoke with a look of it is just beer.

The servant put down the carafe and proceeded to one of the doors.

"Try to get six or more so then you will not have to keep bothering the hotel staff." Christine smiled at him.

Chris Crase

So as the vampires waited for the beer to arrive, Morgan inquired Christine for a cigarette. As Christine handed him her pack he gave her a wink of approval. Morgan then kicked back into his chair and lit up his tobacco and relaxed for he knew that his role of support for Christine was no longer required. Five minutes had passed and the anxiety was starting to take its toll on the room as the hustle and bustle and whispers grew more ramped. Even the council members were uneasy except for Haden who just sat there quietly eyeing Christine who just eyed "hi" back through her smoke glazed wall. By and by the servant returned with a lager. The beer came in bottle served in a bucket of ice that the wait staff supplied. Christine thank the servant with a devilish grin and popped open a bottle and took a swig.

Haden began the interrogation; he propped his elbows unto the table and interlocked his fingers. His brow lowered to conceal Christine from the view of his mouth.

"Christine... we all have heard the tale of you and our lost friend Jarred, and this worker..." he looked to the right of him at another councilman for correctness, "Leif?, and as you know," looking back at Christine, "once a story has been told and passed along by word of mouth to them and to me that story can and will change. I am sure that my version of the story is somewhat of the King James and yours is probably a Martin Luther and others hold a John Smith's version or Calvinist, New International perhaps. So Christine if you would go over the story one more time to clarify ourselves.

Christine kinda laid back and mulled over how t begin her tale.

"Okay let me start at the beginning, I moved to L.A. after a little stint here and there. I set up my usual routine of weekend ladies night out, nothing out of the norm really. Then one night I met this guy at this club who had no earthly business being there. We talked and had an interesting introduction. I wasn't interested in... ah lets see... um well... feeding on him because he wasn't my type. So I went about my business that night and had a tasty little kid. Well then I ran into him again and had a great time, but like I said he wasn't my type so I just enjoyed his company. We kept hanging out and finally I could not resist myself and I kissed him. Little beknownst to me Jarred had been in town and was voyuering over us. Since I almost fell in trouble with the council a couple of centuries ago, Jarred basically forbade the relationship. Looking at it from his perspective and drawing upon my forth said relationship, I figured he was right and I was more than likely infatuated. By and by I did what Jarred asked me to do, I got this man drunk and took him back to his place. When he passed out I bit him. Good blood by the way. Anyhow I thought the deed was done and even though I was sadden by it I went back to my regular life. Well then I ran into him again and it scared the hell out of me. I was taken aback by him still strolling about and then I rationalized that since I had feelings for him that I did not suck hard enough. I began to worry that I had started to change him into a lord which would have gotten me into more trouble. I was busy hanging out with Leif trying to determine if that was the case when Jarred like a guardian angel confronted Leif and I. Jarred immediately attacked Leif and from what I saw completed the task that I was not able to. On a side note, Jarred was ticked off because he thought I was making Leif into one of us without your permission and like I said that is a whole other can of worms. Also I think Jarred had a thing for me. But after Jarred killed Leif we were discussing Leif's enigma when he popped up, turned into a werewolf, which I thought was just some character from old 1950 movies that were in bad taste. I was so shocked that I did not help Jarred, I just stood there while Leif pretty much destroyed Jarred with ease. Then Leif took off."

Haden began with the barrage of questions that followed from nameless faces.

"Do you think Leif is still in town?"

"I do not know, he is very proficient at pretty much everything so he doesn't need to stay around."

"We heard you still see him."

"Do not believe everything you hear."

"Can you see him."

"I do not know."

"But you could contact him."

"I do not know if he is even still here."

"Does he love you?"

"I do not think he could now."

"Does he hate you?"

"Maybe."

"So you are not seeing him now?"

"No."

"There are still reports that you are."

"Like I said don't believe..."

"What do we do with him." this question being directed toward everyone.

"Can we get to him?"

"I do not know."

"She will have to contact him."

Chris Crase

Haden interrupted the inquisition after patiently eyeing Christine and her reactions. "Do you love him?"

Silence fell upon the lords as everyone turned the eyes to her answer. Christine was trapped in uneasiness. "I do not know, I guess, I mean in retrospect I was in love with him."

"I asked you do you love him."

"Like I said I did not even know werewolves existed. With the past incident which was horrible, but then I never experienced it so I cannot understand fully..."

"You do love him."

Thinking it over while staring at the floor, Christine finally answered. "No, I do not love him." sounding exhausted.

And with that the council seemed satisfied. Haden directed the councilmen to form search parties if you will to determine Leif's status. Christine then supplied the lords with a biography of Leif which could have been written by a high school student that had a paper due the next day 10 pages long and only one index card completed on the subject.

Chapter 29

After the meeting and the lords abandoned the social scene into the night for some fun, Christine hung around drinking some beer with Morgan at the hotel bar.

"Kudos to you Christine." Morgan raising his pint glass to her.

"Why thank you very much." and they both had a chuckle.

"I just hope this guy is worth the ruse you gave us."

"Oh do not worry I just gave Leif some time to work his plan out."

"What is his plan?"

"Hell if I know or if he even knows, but what is funny about this guy is that one can always tell that he is figuring something out. His plan will probably just spawn out of his head when the time is right."

"Leif comes off as a weird person."

"Tell me about it. Just the other day he told me that he was going to figure out a way for men to give birth just so the sexes could have equality."

"Okay that is pretty weird."

"That is just the tip of it."

"So what is it about him that you like so much that is different from me?" Morgan beginning to surface past memories.

"Oh, Morgan do not bring up that old stuff, it is like this. I became infatuated with you way back when because you were a vampire. When you came into my life, I fell in love with being with and being someone different that was beyond, I thought, the suffering of the world. I mean you were immortal and free from the day to day goings of the world that is what I loved. At least when looking back we were able to become friends because I would have hated having a bad break up for 700 years."

"I can agree with that." as Morgan smirks and holds his pint glass up again for a toast. "So again I ask you, what do you see in this guy?"

"He is goofy. And he has a lot of fun with life. He keeps exploring it like a wide eyed dreamer as almost he is abusing his life. I guess he awoke me into life and now I want to find out about it again with him."

"Ah, my friends, I thought everyone had transcended out into the city." Haden interrupting the two the two bar flies. "May I join you two while I await my traveling companion to return?" Haden shrouded the surprised Christine.

"Of course you can Lord Haden." Morgan intervened, "What would you like?"

Haden moving to a stool so that Christine is the center of attention. "Ah let us see" perusing the liquor, "What are you having tonight?"

Chris Crase

"Just a few brews." Christine responding.

"I shall have one of those then. I had not had a beer in ages. In fact I have not had one since I became a lord." Smiling smugly.

"And when was that?" Morgan inquiring as he lit up a smoke.

"Lets see... I would imagine around six thousand years ago give or take a few hundred."

"That is a long time to go without a beer." Morgan replied.

"Hah! I suppose it is a very long time. Please, a toast if you will."

"A toast for what?" Christine interjected.

"Why a toast for our reunion. I have not had so many friends together for such a long time. We really need to convene more often. Under better circumstances of course." Haden raised his glass.

Christine and Morgan raised theirs as well and as the clinking of the glasses occurred Christine felt the hand of Haden on her shoulder. Christine shuddered on the inside as she felt his cold smugness run her spine. Quickly taking her drink of beer, she put down the bottle and turned in her chair to grab her smokes of course this resulted in Haden's hand falling off her body. Swinging around again and blowing smoke, by accident, into Haden's face, Christine offered a smoke to the two gentlemen. Morgan took one. Haden on the other hand became sheepish and waved his hand in front of his chest.

"No, no thank you, I have not had a cigarette in a long time. You two have already made me have a beer and now you want me to continue on this path of vices."

Smiling at the two as if he was the fun loving uncle who had just straightened up his act of mischief. Christine made nothing of his remark and set the smokes back onto the bar.

"So what is the errand that your servant is running?" Morgan asked.

"Oh, I have heard from other lords about a particular scotch at a particular store in this city. So I had my servant about locating some cases. Oh yes he is also getting some fresh fruit as well. You would think in such a lavish hotel they could have acquired some decent fruit but alas my cries have gone unanswered."

"Why do you need so much scotch?" Christine sustaining the dull socializing.

"You know one of the lords back home asked me for one then another asked then another and then I figure a case would come in handy for engagements and gatherings. You can never have too much of a good thing."

"Are you sure of that?" Morgan leaning onto the bar.

"What is that?" Haden looking dumfounded.

"Never having too much of a good thing."

Never Fall in Love with a Vampire. It is a Pain in the Neck

"Did I say that? I guess I did. Sometimes I am known to not think before I speak. To answer your question, yes I am sure of that."

"No matter what the cost?" Morgan pushing the lord.

"Yes." Haden said with confidence. "And now I have to bid you two adieu for it looks as if my traveling companion has returned. Thank you both for keeping me quite entertained." Haden exits stage left.

"Is it just me Morgan or does Haden come off like a smuck?"

"Haden is very… umm what is a good word for it, ostentatious."

"Smuck."

"Pretentious?"

"Smuck."

"Snotty?"

"Smuck."

"Yep, smuck is probably the best word to describe him."

"Cheers!"

And by and by, Christine and Morgan had a good time down at the bar with laughter and what not abounding. For good measure, Haden put his servant on an observation role that night of Christine. And as Haden made his way to his room to qualify his merchandise, he made his wishes known to his servant and asked him on the success of the acquisition. After speaking shortly with his servant, Haden seemed very pleased and made his way to the elevator whistling. He arrived at his floor with a new tune and greeted everyone along the way down the corridor. Opening the door to his makeshift home, the hall light revealed a young petite girl sitting, maybe sixteen.

"Well hello there, I am Lord Haden and my servant was right, I am very pleased to meet you Miss…?"

"Sarah."

"Sarah, ah what a lovely name" as Haden proceeded toward the balcony where upon a set of roses stood in a vase upon a corner table.

"Look your friend or servant said you will pay me very well to stay here tonight."

"Quite right, do not be alarmed young one about the payment you are in good hands."

"Well then," Sarah seeming quite content with Haden, "Where should we begin?" as the harlot began to undress.

"Actually, I would like to draw you before we resume the night. It is a fetish of mine but if you would indulge me and perhaps stand over here in the light without your clothes."

"I guess I do not have a problem with that if you tell me what a fetish is."

Chris Crase

Haden was proceeding with removing his art tools from their case, "Well my sweet a fetish is something a person finds pleasurable to oneself, kinda like eating cookies in bed."

Sarah continuing to take her clothes off, "I like eating cookies in bed" with a blushing smile.

Haden disappears into a darken closet with the following words, "I too enjoy eating cookies in bed. Perhaps I will retrieve some for the both of us later."

A few seconds of fumbling, Haden reappears from the closet with a dark green nightgown.

"I had picked this out the night before last and I think you would look lovely on you." bringing the night gown to Sarah.

As he helps her into the gown she replies, "A gift for your wife?"

A little laugh insinuates from Haden, "No child, I am not married. There now." stepping back from Sarah, "Beautiful."

Haden retrieves his utensils and lies back onto the bed. One hand props up the sketch pad while the other gently grasps his ink pen. A hour goes by as he traces out the girl onto his paper. Making light conversation with her during his fetish to ease her, Haden begins to deeply engross himself into his hand. Moving over the paper with particulars to the young child's face and underdeveloped breasts. Besides being a vampire, Haden is quite skilled at the art of inking. He presses on using the lighting in his head to retrieve the depths of the drawing. Paying more attention now to the neck and the thighs, he begins to add teeth marks to around these areas and thus by doing so he stamps his signature upon the work. He sets it aside and beckons young Sarah over to him.

"May I see myself Lord Haden?"

"In the morning my sweet, right now we have pressing matters to attend to."

Sarah in a seductive immature voice, "It is about time."

Haden whispers back to her as she falls onto him, "Oh my child, have not you heard the saying, all good things to those who wait?"

Thus our voyeuristic eyes are darkened by the end of this scene.

Chapter 30

A few weeks of giving Haden's servant the adoring task of tailing Christine, she felt it was safe enough to see Leif. Christine had managed throughout the week to let the servant trail her till dawn sometimes, other nights she would lose him immediately, still others she would lead him on and then ditch him only to reappear hours later to be followed once more. This night she lost him immediately. She knew Leif's local hangout on a Wednesday night and figured on surprising him down there at the local college pubs. It was early and she might be waiting around awhile, so Christine made the best of it. She sat at the edge of the bar entertaining some men and dismissing others. A usual college scene really: the guys would come up to her with pretty much the same lines of introduction, the studies game, the year game, and the friends game. Christine would discuss with some the history classes, others she would talk of feminism,, philosophy, art, math, and even though she would never profess it to herself: Christine was very astute in all subjects not to mention social interaction. The years had taught her how to present herself among the different social circles that befell her. Two hours had whisked by and Christine was engaged into the topic of morality with a suitor.

"What do you mean that there is no right or wrong?" The man exasperates unto Christine's last statement.

"All I am saying is that here and now the distinction between right and wrong cannot be so easily obtained." Christine takes a drink.

"You are telling me that when a man commits a crime he should not be punished?"

"Well, first you have to obtain his guilt and even though that is not popular anymore it still must be sought out if the man committed the crime and then one has to ascertain the crime to determine if it was a crime to begin with."

"Okay, okay now once that man has been convicted of a wrong then he should be punished to the fullest extent of the law."

"Well first you should have to determine if it is a wrong and then decide what the punishment should be."

"The law should say an eye for an eye."

"Nah, I disagree with you. That is only propagating the act."

"How can you say that it provides a deterrence to others with the same motivation."

Chris Crase

"The deterrence is the motivator. In a society where we cannot distinguish between the crime and the punishment, that society is destined to suffer its laws."

"I cannot believe you."

"Think about it why does the law exist. We set up laws based on the framework of the society around it. The society must create the situation that the law must be made. Society demands these laws to protect itself from its creation more than likely cause they cannot own up to their sins of living it. It would be interesting to see if a lawless society could be made. The results might be surprising."

"Now you are beginning to irritate me."

"That is my girl." I interject behind the shoulder of Chris.

"Pard me" The suitor steps back.

"Oh do not mind me, I was listening for awhile. My name is Leif by and by."

"Hey Leif" Chris smiles at me.

"Do not worry my friend, she is always irritating me." smiling at Chris. "Now if will excuse us, Chris I have a table in the back if wish to accompany me."

So we dismissed the scene among glaring looks to the back of the bar whereupon I was with Timmy, Jimmy, Scotty, and the Prof. On the way there I pulled Chris aside to explain the circumstances.

"What are you doing here?" I asked in surprised joy.

"I was able to get away and I knew you would be here thus I figured I would come down and join you."

"I am glad to see you but I have to tell you that my friends are here as well."

"Your college buddies?"

"No, my friends."

"Oh, should I leave?"

"Nah I want you to meet them actually I have been dying to introduce you to them. I just want to make sure you are comfortable."

"Well, I am not since you asked but I will come along."

"Not to worry they are good chaps, a little misbehaved, but all in all good. Besides I will be right there with you." Continuing our movement to the table.

"Oh that makes me fell much better." Chris says with a smirk.

And so I retired to retrieve the beer that the guys ordered me to get and followed Chris back to the table of friends amide an every growing crowd.

"Everyone, this is Christine." I announced to the pack.

Never Fall in Love with a Vampire. It is a Pain in the Neck

One by one each greeted her. The Prof and Timmy were warm welcoming Chris whereas understandably Jimmy and Scotty were snooty but remained hospitable.

"Where did you go to get that beer? Canada?" Scotty trying his best to make his best conversation.

Jimmy sat back and lit a cigarette, eyeing Chris with an ever so present glare. Sitting Chris in my chair, I was busy about locating another to bring to the table.

"Well shit Scotty this is somewhat of a busy night." Grinning at him "Besides I had to save Chris here from a mob of gentlemen."

"So this is one of your college hangouts Leif?" The Prof speaking up "Is this were you two met?"

Chris fielding the answer while I was still looking for a damn chair, "Actually no we met down on the strip. I was out gallivanting around looking for a… well gallivanting around when this creep came up to me and proceeded to throw every line in the book, and then some, at me and, by and by, pawing me at the same time."

Timmy injected, "So our good Samaritan Leif came by and got rid of this clown right?"

"No on the contrary, I was talking about Leif."

Silence fell on the group before the Prof got the humor and began laughing. Even Jimmy posed a little smirk from the remark.

"Ha, ha everyone have a good laugh at my expense" I said.

"I kinda figured that is what happened," Scotty taking a shot, "Leif has always had the way with the women."

"That's right." Timmy broke in, "I remember this time when Leif and I were in New York and he was whispering sweet nothings into this girl's ear all night long. He was drunk of course. Anyway I do not know what he said to this girl but she proceeded to get up with her friend. She had that look in her eye of wanting towards the Leifer and went to the ladies room. She took her friend which I was making some headway with. So as they were gone we toasted each other for our probables and exchanged stories about what we liked about them. To cut a long story short we waited till closing for the ladies to come back."

"If I remember right Timmy you were the one who was willing to give up everything for that girl and follow her around like a lost puppy." Breaking the roast.

"You too."

"That is besides the point." Laughter ensues and as it dies down Chris was growing impatient with my standing around looking for a chair.

"Here Leif sit down and I will get a chair."

Chris Crase

"Huh, oh, well Chris I cannot get a chair; they are all being used."

"Hold on I will be right back." Chris leaves with a smirk.

"Going to the ladies room?" Scotty kicking the dead horse but actually got a laugh.

"I am going to get a chair." Chris makes her way to a table of college guys.

About thirty seconds later, Chris returns with a chair that was being saved for one of the college guy's girlfriends. All is fair in love and war. And then if I wasn't a dog by nature, Chris went and got us another round. She did not do this to win the guys over by any means, she did it cause she is Chris. When she rejoined us a second time, Chris lit a smoke. I changed the subject from a roast.

"Hey by and by, I was at the coffee place today talking to a few chaps when one of them spoke up and said my name was contrived. Talk about being thrown where I have never thought so. I have been carrying that around all day as well as that stupid new song on the radio. You know the one, 'And mmm – mm – mmm – mmm.' I cannot get that out of my head either. Anyway have you guys ever been told that your name is contrived?"

"Nope."

"Negative good buddy"

"Nah"

"Well I have a nickname of a doctor of something but even then I never had it received as being contrived."

"I was told last week at a bar by a couple of snobbish accountants that were hitting on me." Chris answers.

"I mean what the heck is that all about?" I am going to rant now, "How can a person's name be contrived? It's not like I chose this name, it was giving to me by my creators. I had no say. I mean I guess one could say that to my creators cause they chose the name and maybe it is contrived then but you cannot address the person who had no say in the matter about it. And even then it would be more rude to address the creators about it than me because it is like telling a parent that their child is ugly. Plus what is the big whoop about it anyway? All Leif is is a proper noun used to distinguish myself against another contrived name," Looking at Chris, "What really counts is the character defined."

"Here, here!" the Prof raises his glass is approval.

"Same ol'Leif" Jimmy adds on as the toast ensues.

"So you are saying that every name in contrived?" Timothy continuing.

"I do not know."

"Is there any name that is not?" Jimmy starts in.

"Beats the vittles out of me." Said I.

Never Fall in Love with a Vampire. It is a Pain in the Neck

"God." Christine intercedes "I guess God wouldn't be, it may be a little vain or egotistical"

"True, true" The Prof spoke.

Enter Morgan unseen in the back of us.

"Well that just opens up a whole new can of worms doesn't it." Scotty states.

"I guess we just cannot win but to be cliche, a rose by any other name is still…" I begin.

"Boo"

"Yeah, boo!"

"Hiss"

Laughing I said, "Oh you know it was coming, I was setting everything up so well."

Laughter.

"Evening Christine," Morgan broke the laughter by shocking Chris and the rest of us for that matter.

"Morgan!?" bewildered, Chris glances the bar for any other lords abounding. She gets up to greet him with a hug.

Hugging, Morgan whispers, "Not to worry Chris, I am alone."

"Are you sure?"

"Yep." breaking apart, "May I join you? I have this pitcher of beer and no one to drink it with."

Idiots that we were just stared at him for a spell until Chris nudged me.

"Oh yes of course you can. Here take my chair and Chris you can sit on my lap."

So there, a very uncomfortable scene is created.

"I am Leif by the way" extending my hand.

"Leif!?" Morgan greets my hand with his. "Christine gave me the impression that you were taller."

"It is the hair." trying to break the ice, "Let me introduce you." As I sat down with Chris on top. I could feel her nerves or were these mine. "This is Timmy, my best friend, Jimmy, Scotty, and the Prof."

"How do you do?" Morgan extending his hand which was greeted by a nod from Jimmy and Scotty, the Prof shook which prompted Timmy to give a quick shake of the hand but he would have preferred a nod as well.

"And judging by Chris's reaction, you are Morgan."

"Yes that is right," Morgan filling his glass. "Can I top off anyone?"

I pushed Chris's and mine ahead to be filled and lit a smoke. Chris motioned to me a cig.

Well if this is not an awkward situation, I do not know what is awkward. Morgan topped off our beers and sat calmly at the table lighting his own

Chris Crase

cigarette. The Prof kinda sat back examining the situation and a delightful look came over his face. I swear he was just so amused with it all.

"So is everyone having a good time tonight? It looks as if this place is a hopping." Morgan inquired.

"Yeah, I usually frequent this place on this night being a student and all." I entertained the question.

"That is right you are a college man now aren't you Leif."

"Yep, trying to become a doctor or at least the piece of paper."

"Are you enjoying yourself then?"

"It is an interesting adventure."

"What made you do it?"

"Lack of anything better to do really and partly because I have always been fascinated by it." Dragging my smoke. "So I figure I would try."

"It sounds like you are taking life by the stirrups, almost as if you have not a second to lose. And yet you seemingly have all the time in the world."

"Ummm, yes and no."

"How do you mean?"

"Well, not really bringing up the situation, but we all pretty much have eternity."

"True"

"But, but we won't always have right now, sure I could always do this but times change, things change so it would never be quite like this moment. So yes I am taking life by the stirrups and doing the best to hang on."

"Now that is what I get from Christine, and it is very interesting. I myself you see have pretty much laid in content, doing everything the same day in and day out or I guess night in and night out. Sure I move to a different locale but still..."

"Night in and night out." Scotty spoke smugly.

"I have to use the restroom." Jimmy got up and removed himself.

"I think I will join you." Scotty got up and followed.

"Boy did a cold breeze just flow through here or is it just me?" Morgan stating.

The Prof speaks up, "I would not say cold Morgan just unexpected. This is not easy for any of us you know and some us as I am sure on your end as well still have bitter feelings."

"Ja, do not take it too..." I was saying.

"I think I will go and check on the guys." Timmy announced.

"Ah, Timmy do not leave the night is still young and I was going to introduce you to some girls."

"Nah, I better make sure they are all right."

"Timmy."

Timmy leaves.

"Let him go Leif." The Prof states.

"Anyhow Morgan as Leif begun to say do not take it too personally." The Prof says satirically sullen.

Chris gets up and moves to one of the empty chairs.

"Not to worry Leif, I would not have come down here if I was not ready for a reception like that. However, I must say I am sad cause they seemed like interesting fellows."

"So where do we go from here?" Chris asks.

"I do not know. I just came down here to hang out. All this stuff the others are doing was driving me crazy. Always asking me about Christine and Leif and what I know I just needed a break." Morgan pronounced. "So if we can lighten the mood a bit."

"Here, here!" I lifted my glass. "I say we get piss drunk and raise some hell!"

"Always looking for a good time Leif is." as the Prof lifted his up followed by Chris and Morgan.

By and by the next hour was filled with comical tales of our youths before we became immortalized. The Prof told us of his family he had in the wild wild west trying to reach California but gave up and opted for New Mexico. His trail of wagons gave up just a the foot of rocks they would have to cross. Tales were told of haphazard farming and the old towns long since gone. This is when the Prof decided to turn in his farm and bruised green thumb into a commune for lost souls in particular the young.

Morgan entertained us with his thoughts of the fall of Rome and why the Romans alcohol was much better than today's standards. He had one hilarious tale of his times in Carthage when he drank too much and wound up on a Roman Naval boat heading for Athens. The months ensuing, Morgan had learned the ropes of sailing but mostly washed the deck and cut food for the sailors of which he did not compare too much physically. He still had the hands of young swashbucklers, who's tale is not far off from many figures in literature. Morgan was turning out to be an all right fella, and even the Prof was enjoying his company. It might have been the alcohol of course but still I kept my hopes up.

The night went on with drunkenness and even the scene I think made the two lords with us drunk with delight. More stories were told, cigarettes smoked, and alcohol consumed. We started to play really old cheesy music on the jukebox. You know the music described as cheese: the songs we grew up with singing all day long and never missing a beat. However, as the age takes on and the tastes change we can all reflect on some songs as "What the hell was I thinking" when we hear them again.

Chris Crase

And thus I went to the bar to order yet another couple of unneeded pitchers of beer, and it began. The young men that Chris was entertaining until my arrival had become a little surly and a lot drunker as they do. They began in their only sarcastically manner to debase me. I take it all in stride though knowing that it is expected to happen just as it does over and over. My ignorance of their pretense however was my downfall for as I began to carry the pitchers back to the table, I was confronted by a group of one of the many suitors and his cronies. A few remarks were made and they had to make an extra effort to make them. They kept leaving themselves open for smart barks of my own wit, which I guess agitated them more and more. What could I do it was so easy to drown them in their idiot antics. So before I could give a smirk the pitchers were knocked out of my hands (what a waste by and by) and I caught a 1,2 to the gut and then the jaw. I fell idly by to the wall amid other standing folks.

All eyes fixed upon my reaction, so I just laid their fishing in my pocket for a lighter and a smoke. The ruffians yelled down remarks of the manhood while I lit my bent cig and the rest of the bar joined in egging on the fight.

As soon as the voices raised they fell as Chris approached the group of men. The leader whom was one of the guys she talked to earlier asked smugly.

"Finally realized who is worth hanging out with, eh?"

"No."

Smartly (not really of course) he fires back at me.

"Oh I see you have to get your girl to save you huh?"

His friends laughed, why I do not know, so I said.

"She is her own woman. I have nothing over her actions but from what I can tell she is about to thrash you."

"Oh I am so scared."

Actually he did not finish his sentence because Chris proceeded to give him a 1,2,3 which is a shot to the nose, then the gut, then the other spot that every man dreads. Laying about a foot away from me I offered him a smoke as Chris' heel dug in his neck.

"Anyone else?" Chris addressed the guy's group.

So I offered the other guy who was now lying next to me a smoke as well.

"Now the way I figure it, you guys owe us some beer." Chris stated to the remaining members. But alas as is bar fights the violence grew as other brewing problems erupted around us. Chris and I retreated to a corner to watch the action. We were in luck, the corner had two fresh bottles of beer, so we helped ourselves as the brawl continued. My eye caught Morgan and the Prof get into the action as they tried to break up a group of pugilists. As they pulled the fighters apart, Morgan was plowed into by friends of the person in his grasps. And as the gang pounced him, I saw the Prof break the pile with a stool that broke onto three or four backs. He helped Morgan up and cracked a smile as they threw their arms around each other's shoulder and made their way over to us. The bouncers, owners, bartenders, and finally the cops broke up the brawl as we stood outside on the sidewalk. Of course, Chris and I had some explaining to do but it was amid our groups laughter at the night.

Chapter 31

One night Chris stopped by my apartment just after dusk. I was busy studying or better stated I was putting off studying any means possible; tonight it was an old film rerun on TV that I had only seen 129 and a half times through. After the movie I had figured on getting some coffee and smokes at the coffee shop and put off studying even more so. So we went down to the coffee shop. A typical scene for the shop, just a bunch o cats hanging to key muzak in a Havana fog. "Get me a choco stick" I said to myself. We grabbed a table amongst the crowd thus starting the following dialog.

"So there is some stuff that I have been wondering about you Chris?" propping one elbow on the circular table with its perspective fist holding my chin.

"What do you want to know?" sipping her mocha.

"Well we all have heard the myths and stories about you lords, I just would like to know what it is like to be one. A lord that is."

"Okay, what would you like to know?"

"Garlic?"

"Love it, especially on pizza."

"Hmmmmm, Crosses?"

"Tacky symbol, especially when has Jesus depicted on them, I don't need that for faith."

"Okay, Holy water?"

"Irritating, I hate getting wet unnecessarily"

"Sunlight?"

"Very irritating."

"Can change into a bat."

"Nope."

"Malicious?"

"Depends on the lord."

"Death by stake though the heart?"

"Anything that severs the flow of blood from the heart, the heart is the key."

"Can you fly?'

"Yes."

"Now way!! That is so cool."

"It's fun."

"So the religious stuff like crosses and holy water do not affect you?"

"Nope"

Never Fall in Love with a Vampire. It is a Pain in the Neck

"Huh, I would have figured that is why you are religious."

"Nah Leif, if you think about it that is kinda ludicrous. I mean then you would have the lords in the middle east fearing some other idols and taboos and the same in Asia and what not. It would be to complicated to keep track of it all."

"So then why are you religious."

"I just have a sense of something going on bigger than myself ya know. I would not call it religious but rather existential"

"I hear ya and that is cool but to change the subject lets talk about flying"

"What about it?"

"What is it like?"

"Flying is like… flying."

"Huh?"

"Well it is a wonderful sense of freedom. You know how people say sometimes I wish I could just fly away."

"Yeah"

"Well I can."

"That is too cool" taking a chug of my joe and lighting a smoke. Suddenly my thoughts became more grave, I don't know why they just do. "What about the blood thing?"

"What about it?" Chris getting a little uneasy.

"I mean what is the deal with vamps and blood?"

"Well we kinda need it to live, once you become a vampire it is like a virus that enters the blood. I do not know the science around it I just know that we need fresh blood to keep us going. That is why a stake through the heart kills us. We can no longer pump the blood."

"So do you need to take humans every night?"

"Oh, no, we can last several days,, months without it, I have gone months actually. It is not pleasant though, we get tired and sick."

"How about human blood do you need only human blood or will animals work?"

"I have heard that animals, particular ones only can provide sufficiently for us."

"Does it bother you, taking a life?"

"Ah, it is something I really choose not to think about."

"Why?"

"Well it just becomes frustrating, on one end we need to survive and on the other hand like you said it is taking a life. There is the animal factor but like I said it revolves around specific ones so there is possibility of extinction of the species whereas humans continue on, and as we have seen

Chris Crase

they will continue on. It use to bother more when I first became a lord but now I push it out of my head."

"It does not bother you as much now."

"Well as of late it has become a question, just around when I met you in fact you have started to get me wary of the human spirit once again. Now it is not that easy. I have a renewed appreciation for humans so it is making it harder. Shit, Leif it is hard ya know it is not like I am judgmental of them like they are on themselves. I pick and choose with no bias I just do what it takes to live. I am happy about that, I do not possess the qualitative characteristic of judge, jury, executioner, if it was like that then my life would be harder. It is hard enough."

"Interesting where man has taken upon itself to decide whether this life or that life is important you can skip all that and get right to point as if ridding yourself of the initial question, and man will ever ponder its meaning."

"In a way but I wonder if they even ponder it anymore."

"Well then allow me to offer myself as your life source. It doesn't affect me and then I can help you alleviate your albatross."

"You would do that?"

"Sure, why not. Besides, I know you guys prefer our blood because it gives that extra kick, so I figure as long as no one is getting hurt. And if you grow tired of it then we will work out something else. Another thought, Chris do you miss the sun?"

"Very much so, sometimes I do not sleep during the day. I will just lay in bed looking through the curtains at the daylight and wonder what is happening. Imagining all those people getting up every day against the morning to do what I have no idea. To feel the sun on my face on top of a grassy knoll like I did when I was a kid. Sunsets, high noon, lunch, all of it is something I have lost. Time though has healed that longing, I have been accustom to the night now so the day goes by as they say day in day out."

"Hmm, I guess we are both creatures of the night yours by law almost and mine by a choice."

"So anyway," lighting her own cig and grinning at me with cat eyes.

"What?" goofy.

"I gave now you divulge. What is it like being a worker?"

"Well besides the fleas, the uncontrollable urge to sniff crotches, the pain of walking close to fire hydrants; I really love getting my ears scratched."

"Funny but really, what is it like?"

"It is kinda what you were saying about freedom. In a way I am of nature whereas a human and a lord perhaps would think of nature as a burden or that they are the top of the food chain, I belong to it; we, being the worker and nature, grow together feeling each others harmony and all to recently our pain."

"Do you hunt then?"

"Ah, I tried it a couple of times, really did not enjoy it. I mean I have taken life of a deer before but I did not take to it. I do not need to do it to survive so I figure why bother. Some us enjoy the hunt, that is why most are scattered in packs in remote areas of the world where the hunt is good and away from prying eyes. I was on this gala once up north with a pack a few decades ago. We whooped it up around the camp fire and then took off with the intent of ya know pack hunting. I just could not handle it when they brought down that caribou. All in celebration, the glory, something I cannot appreciate especially when I realize nature has enough problems surviving without our intervention so I leave the hunting to the real wolf, he needs it more than I do. However, I do get the criticisms from the others but I do not mind it."

"I think I understand what you are saying. So how did you become a worker?"

Chapter 32

Yeah, so it happened about two hundred years ago. I was living on a farm with my folks in the Northeast just enjoying life. I fucked around for the most part breaking my father's farm equipment by trying to make things. He never really cared though cause he was guilty of the same thing. The only time he became agitated was when I beat him to a piece of machinery that he had aspirations for. The days were spent trying to make the stuff of stuff work with my friend Timothy who was a local merchant slash trader. He made quite a good living importing and exporting always looking for the big pay off. He usually was screwed over because most of the deals were made in the black market or some other creep of capitalism.

I would always show up at his shop to see what new things he got in from around the world. After he closed shop we headed for the inn. With the same drinks in hand we would hang with the locals or sometimes go to the inns at the docks and hang with the pirates and sailors. Sometimes the pirates would throw a party on the boat and we would divulge our presence. One time we merried it up too much and woke the next morning on the way to Cuba. Luckily we were able to convince the first mate to drop us off somewhere in Virginia and by and by made it home. All right it was more than one time and yes we did make it to Cuba.

Young Timothy was a man of the world and he would entertain me with stories of grandeur and mystery. He taught me to read and write and soon discovered that most of his tales came from a book. Imagine the disappointment when I read Robinson Crusoe not to mention The Canterbury Tales. But alas he did have plenty of tales of his own of which he would bolster to the maidens at the inns we would woo.

And so it happened one weekend when I had the farm to myself wielding the awesome power of imagination with it. I was planning my greatest invention yet: the fertilizer transponder monolith. For weeks I had been plotting and scheming the greatest farming invention that would make me rich beyond all belief. The concept was to use running water to turn my wheels in precise order to in urn turn the shredder. After the shredder was the disperser which was really a makeshift catapult that I stole from ancient England warfare. The idea was to take useless crop, dirt, trees, manure, and whatever and to "mulch" the components together and then to hurl the "mulch" over the fields thus producing a food for the crops making them the best in the world. I was also working on my sun collector to intens

Never Fall in Love with a Vampire. It is a Pain in the Neck

By and by I had told Timothy to show up around threeish and I would show him my new toy. He arrived with great anticipation for he new I was plotting something big cause I had been somewhat withdrawn and busy for the last week.

"So young Leif, what is this new invention."

"A revolutionary farming idea that will change the world and feed pretty much all of it."

"Does it work?"

"I don't know I have not turned it on."

"Well young squire how will it make us the richest men in the world if you don't have it on?"

"I was waiting for you to show up so I can share the glory."

"Well then let us begin our rich man's life."

"Yes, come with me it is in the barn."

"Where are your folks?"

"They went down south to see me uncle's new kid."

"Ah, so how are they."

"They do well."

"That is why you have been so busy, with your dad gone you had free reign over all his stuff."

Grinning, "Yep he won't like what I have done one bit."

Opening the doors to the barn I revealed the monster that I created. Timothy looked up in awe of the greatest invention and thus saying "Oh yeah, your dad is going to be mad."

"It has taken me months to build, hiding away certain parts here and there not to reveal the extent of my machine."

"Well enough standing around and looking at it not running, turn it on Leif." Timothy tossing his coat to the corner and rolling up his sleeves for he was really seeing the potential of it as well. I quickly ran to the back of the barn where I had attached my aqueduct to the river. Quickly glancing over the contraption and verifying all the stuff was in order I yelled out to Timothy, "Okay I am ready!"

"Turn it on!"

And with that I release the lever and the water started to flow expeditiously down onto the wheels. It was working! I ran to join Timothy who was as shocked as me.

"Okay now what?" he inquired.

"Help me throw this trash into the shredder!"

"Right!"

We hastily threw and threw all the trash I had collected around the farm into the shredder. This is where the shit hit the fan. Even though everything else was working the shredder needed some work on the design. I don't remember much after that except that beam was heading down from the rafters onto Timothy and I had no time to think as I pushed him to safety outside the barn. The rafter hit me and then the rest of the fertilizer transponder monolith hit me. I believe when Timothy found me I was bleeding internally and had not much time to live, that is when Timothy decided my fate and I remember slightly transforming into what I would become and he knelt down and bit me. So now I am a worker and have been making more trouble since.

Chapter 33

We left the coffee shop to explore the avenues and what not of the campus. Chris and I just bullshitted the night talking about meaningless things that somehow are the meaningful things. We were walking upon the grasses of the campus and I was showing some of the places that I like to hang out and the places where my classes are held. After perusing the classrooms and the computer clusters and the other buildings, we found ourselves out on the quad once again.

"Now, check this building out Chris," I pointed to one of the libraries, "Now I really enjoy the way this building has been constructed and placed with the rest of the college. Notice the edge that was put there and the way it blends in even though it is newer than the others. And even though it captures it belonging to the scene, it still is different enough with the placement of its glass windows and it's character that it stands there by itself. What do ya think Chris?" I turn to look at response. "Chris?" She wasn't standing next to me so I pulled a 360 glancing the quad to see where she went. "Chris, hello? I don't like talking to myself even though I increasingly find myself doing so. Chris?"

This is when I heard a devilish snicker from above me. I looked up and saw her just a floating away gazing at me with a mischievous look that for some reason only a woman can pull off. "What are you doing?" I smiled at her whale raising my arms to catch her. Like I needed to do that.

"Nothing."

"Well then come down here."

She floated down into my arms and put her arms around me, "Are you ready" smiling at me.

"What? are you going to kiss me?"

"Nope, something better."

And with that Chris grabbed onto me and took off into the night air. We took off quickly due to the fact I believe Chris wanted to shock me which she did. Chris stopped just above the building line of the campus and just began to circle like a vulture.

"You can open your eyes."

"My eyes are not shut; the rest off my face is just flexing cause of the shock that makes it looks like my eye are shut."

"Well quit flexing your face and look."

So I opened my eyes and looked down upon the peons as I was a god among them. Looking around I saw the scurrying of the kids: my academia friends. "What a view!" I said looking around at the university. Everything

Chris Crase

became a new perspective as I saw how all it was working together, the walkways, the fields, the buildings, the benches, the nook and granny. It was brilliant. I looked at Chris as she was smiling at me. "What else can you show me?"

"Hold on."

We took to the city, passing over the streets in a blink watching the cars move along me. My head was a revolving door as I tried to take it all in as fast as my sensory ability would allow. Looking down, looking up I was intoxicated. We got downtown and that is when the fun really started. Chris took me on a roller coaster through the buildings in and around the carved canyons of man. It was fun seeing my reflection in the mirrored windows. Up and down, back and over we sailed through the buildings. More I screamed like a kid on his first trip through Space Mountain. So Chris giggling took me through again, around and around spiraling a building to the top and then over to another building and down in a free fall. That scared me a bit but I was enjoying myself too much to care. And then she took me out towards the direction of the ocean and Charlie's.

"Hey look there is Charlie's." I said as she swooped down to just above the roof and barely skimming the beach we plowed right into the mist of a the sea. We ran out onto the sea as the moonbeams tried to keep up with our flight. I was so close to the water I could dip my hands into the water. Some porpoise caught wince of our flight and joined us on the other side of the looking glass water. "Incredible!" I screamed and just when I thought it was over Chris stopped pulling up about twenty yards from the surface and held me in her arms. She smiled at me then gave me a kiss, we looked like comic book heroes suspended in time and space. And with that she let me go. As I fell into the ocean I thought to myself, "I should have known better." I surfaced, wet to her laughter above me and even the porpoise was splashing around me cackling.

"Now is not the time to tell you I cannot swim?" grinning at her.

"Oh, come on you can doggie paddle can't you."

"Touché" I looked at the porpoise, "How about a lift pal." the porpoise turned around and I grabbed his dorsal and we took off to shore. "Race ya back to Charlie's" I yelled back.

Chris was a little taken back by the porpoise understanding me, so I had the initiative but alas she was able to easily over take me and my friend about three quarters of the way. I left my friend about fifty feet from the shore and swam the rest of the way. I washed up on shore and started to make my way to the bar, rinsing and ringing myself there.

I walked in to see Chris perched up on the barstool chatting with Charlie.

Never Fall in Love with a Vampire. It is a Pain in the Neck

"Leifer!" Charlie exclaimed. "What happened to you?"

"The most incredible thing I ever seen Charlie, I was sitting on the beach minding my own beeswax when all of a sudden a freakish tidal wave struck and hit me."

"Ah, quita pulling my leg. Here sit up here and drink your beer and I will get you some towels."

I sat down next to Chris and she looked at me with devilish eyes and said, "Tidal wave, eh?"

"Don't you start on me too." I laughed.

"Well at least you had a friend to bring you back."

"Yeah, she is a good mate."

"How did the porpoise know what you were saying?"

"Well in a way we are kinda related."

"Is that what you were saying about being of nature?"

"Not really, we have this thing with nature. The dolphins and us used to somewhat of the same thing as far a s the evolution explains it so we have an underlining sense of one another."

"So you can communicate with them?"

"Yeah, and let me tell you how pissed they are at Flipper getting all the attention."

"Oh shit" cracking a grin at me.

Charlie enter with some towels, "So what have ya kids been up to these days? Leifer and Chris, you two are never around anymore!"

"We have been up to no good." Chris tells him.

"Well I kinda figured on that. I just want to know if it isa something you canna tell me."

"We could tell ya Charlie but then will would have to kill ya." I seriously spoke to Charlie.

"Really? Well I'sa don't care for none of then Leifer."

"Oh, he is just yanking your chain Charlie. Leif has been busy with school and I have been stuck at work trying to make the impossible happen."

"What is the impossible you are working on?"

"Trying to look like I am working!"

"Oh yas I always have to do that or the misses isa down my neck." Charlie starts walking back to the kitchen. "Yep she isa always on my back" as the door shuts behind him.

"So what do you want to do now?" Chris turned to me.

"Come on I have an idea."

"What?"

Chris Crase

I got up with Chris following behind me. We walked on to the beach into a dark area where the lights stretched in vain to light the sand but paled by the stars.

Chris smiling, "If you think you are going to get lucky, you are quite mistaking Leif. Leif? Hey Leif where did you go?" Chris tried to pierce through the darkness to see where I had disappeared.

"This ain't cute Leif." Chris said as she began to get a little agitated. Before she could get to mad though she was knock down from the back by myself as only a playful dog would do. And as she lifted her head from the sand and spit out small granules from her mouth she me standing in front of her as a wolf. The stars lit up my gray fur as I looked at her with those stupid grins that we have and my tale wagging.

"Very funny Leif." I thought so. Chris just looked at me in a kinda angry state and then her face changed as she looked over the animal in front of her to shear amazement. I approached her and she reached out her hand to feel my soft fur. Her touch felt could as all dogs know about getting petted but I had other things in mind.

"Try to keep up!" I grinned at her.

And with that I spun around and heading up the pier down the boardwalk and into the city. Chris wasted no time in the chase and immediately took to the air. Christine got a glimpse of me a few blocks away heading down a blank street. She took to a higher plane to keep a better eye on my movement. I weaved in and out of the alleys, scaring some cats out into the light along the way. Over the parking lots I glided along into a residential areas where chained and fence dogs howled me on in jealousy. Back into the alley ways I leapt the fences with a cushion of air beneath my body helping me. Chris started her own prance above me turning and twisting the night air around her body. Into a park I drove though the woods and out into an intersection; cars are the most annoying thing in the street. Where do they get off barreling down my road when I am just running though it. Horns screamed and drivers honked their mouths at me. Whoops!, look out for that one. I could hear Chris laughing above at the spectacle. And then we reached the hills as I climb the hill to meet her height. She skimmed me as I rounded the roof top and into the woods approaching yet another hill. She lost me under the growth of the forest. Chris halted and began to search the area for a moving shadow. She finally caught glimpse of me sitting at the top of the hill on a grassy knoll back into my self. She swooped down and tossed me my clothes as I thanked her. She landed a bit away to give me time to dress.

Running or actual a fast paced jog, Chris came running up to me as I was finishing putting on my soaked shoes. I was not paying real attention

Never Fall in Love with a Vampire. It is a Pain in the Neck

and it was dark so as I was standing clumsily on one foot Chris pushed me over.

"That is not funny." I joked to her.

"What's a matter Leif don't like it when karma bits ya."

"Not at all." laughing.

"Where are we?"

"Oh this is where I like to come to get away." Standing up I took her hand. "Look at the stars, here there is a plethora of them. You can almost reach up and touch them."

It was true the stars on the night sky was immense, a dancing opera. And as Chris looked upward at the grinning constellations; I took her hand and led her over to the brush.

"And no look at these stars." I said as I moved away the branches.

Below was the city shining upward as if it was in a battle with the sky. Chris and I just stood there till almost dawn just watching the life around us. And just as dawn was about to appear, Chris gave me a kiss, good morning, and took of into the air. I stayed a little longer watching the sun rise up destroying the city's stars.

Chris Crase

Chapter 34

The Prof visited me tonight with some disturbing news. Last night some of the chaps of mine got caught in a fuss with some lords. I guess with the multitude of lords and workers in a place, the shit would eventually go down. The Prof explained that it occurred at pretty popular nightclub and considering for the most part both of us like to whoop it up at social gatherings. It was an easy guess that both parties would be there. The Prof was actually there with Jimmy and Scotty. Among about ten other workers as well, they were doing their part to present a showing. According to the Prof, who is not the most aware of a guy at a social scene, the lords about an equal amount began over zealously pushing themselves around agitating Jimmy and the others. Soon words were exchanged and the groups took themselves outside. Luckily enough, the Prof called Marcus and the troops arrived in the middle of the action causing the lords to retreat. Marcus ordered to give chase but alas the lords were able to withdraw. I guess Marcus and the others ended up at a dive celebrating their victory.

Chris called me later that night and told me what she had heard on the grapevine. She described a person who fits Scotty to a T. Scotty was barking out his usual shit in a typical Scotty drunken state at the lords to entice them. The lords pretty much ignored them until he became a little too rowdy and egged on the lords to the outside where Marcus had an ambush waiting for them. I had told Chris the other side of the story and we both agreed that the truth was probably somewhere in between. However, I was very agitated with the actions of Marcus and decided to confront him on the matter.

I arrived at his residence one afternoon unexpected. Cloe answered the door in surprise but treasonous look on her face. I was not in a pleasant mood.

"Marcus is not in." she sneered.

"Do not give me that, I can smell him."

"Well he is busy."

"So am I." I walked by her.

Playing catch up she followed me as I followed my nose.

"He won't see you."

"On the contrary my dear," I opened the door to the room he was in, "I believe he will."

I walked into a room whereupon I saw Marcus and a few other workers sitting about talking.

"Leif, we were just discussing you."

Never Fall in Love with a Vampire. It is a Pain in the Neck

"Well I have some things I would like to discuss."

"Okay what would you like to talk about?"

"Oh no, just you and I. The rest do not need to hear the ass chewing you are going to receive."

Everyone was taken aback by that remark even me; I guess that is what I wanted. They all glanced at Marcus who very calmly stated, "Very well, if all of you will excuse us, Leif and I must talk."

With that the workers reluctantly left the room with Cloe at the end of the trail. She did not say a word just glared. I just gave her the look of "do not fret you are not the first girl to give me that look". However, that look will always send a chill up every man's spine. So with the shut of the door it was just Marcus and me.

"What is on your mind Leif?"

"Your actions the other night whether it was an ambush like Chris described or the rallying of the troops."

"What about my actions?"

"You had the lords retreating, no serious harm done and then you order to chase them down and finish them."

"Yes and what is the problem?"

"Hello? Do you need a clue?" This situation will not be resolved by us trying to eradicate them nor vice versa."

"What do you want from me Leif? You were the one that created this mess and so now I am stuck here in a situation where we have a bunch of lords cornered. Some that I even remember from years ago and we have the upper hand filled and it was filled with angry blood. I could not very well stand down that might have created resentment and splits in the workers."

"But you had won, they were retreating!"

"Leif, you just do not understand. You were not there like the others were. What had it been? 100? 200 years that you have been a worker. You do not know what it was like and you will never know."

"I might get the chance if we do not shape up. You are right though, even with my best imagination, I cannot ever know what you and Logan and the others went through. And I thank you for that because I do not ever want to know. But I do know something Marcus."

"And what is that?"

"This is not about settling some thousands year old blood feud; it is about getting over some thousands year old blood feud. Cause if we don't, this shit is never going to end. If is not me creating the problem it is someone else like Scotty creating a reckless misguided problem. And with that I bid you adieu because it looks like my problem has just grown and I have some work to do."

Chapter 35

I hooked up with Chris again that night; we decided to jump a train that was heading North just for the hell of it. We were down at the train yard looking for one that was about to jet. Alas, the only one was a passenger train so instead of being miscreants we bought tickets and boarded like good citizens. We immediately made our way to the boxcar with the bar and then onto the observation lounge with our drinks. We settled down at the table with the stars shining down through the plexiglass dome. Christine found the daily newspaper and popped it open and was perusing the ins and outs of L.A. I, myself, was busy scribbling down ideas for a replacement of lead shields for X-Rays. My idea was not working so well; thank god, Chris found the opinions and was reading them to me as she picked apart the souls of those who sent them in. What is it about opinion columns being written mostly by idiots of the general populous. For the most part, the editorials are grammatically correct as if the person pained over it for hours ensuring they will be taken seriously. But for all its correctness the authors have failed to bring across meaning, insight, nor answers. But at least it is correct. Correct to the point that all the flare and creativeness is ignored. What is worse is this ideology is used in non-opinionated pieces where the staff of the newspaper itself cannot even write the news without fucking it up. Then there are the ones who lack everything in writing; you know the ones: they always got an "F" on their papers in school as a second grader about their summer vacation. The horrid individuals fill the newspapers with ludicrous, awful, painful writings to the point you cannot in good consciousness leave the paper or book for that matter on the floor of a truck station bathroom, because you would feel you would be desecrating the stall. At least there are some morals in the world. I cried of laughter as Chris made this point in her ramblings.

"By and by Leif, What did Marcus say today?" Christine asked me while gazing out the window at my reflection.

"Not much, I do not feel he is going to help our plight as much as I had hoped."

"So what are you thinking of doing now?"

"I do not know. We have not the big guns helping us but at least we have the Prof and Morgan. Both of them are pretty well respected among our mutual circles."

"You think they will be able to help out?"

"I hope they can, the biggest problem is this Haden bloke. He has influence amongst the lords."

Never Fall in Love with a Vampire. It is a Pain in the Neck

"He does and what is worse is he really does not care for anything but the lords."

"That will be the key hopefully, you and Morgan have to get a strong base against him. If we can do that than I figure we can end this pretty harmlessly."

"Well we will need to find a way to convince some of the council then they will have a good chance to suede the others."

"I find alcohol works well in such situations."

"Well, I shall have to try that method." Chris gave me a wink, "Leif, I was wondering today."

"'Bout what?"

"Well, why do like hanging out with me?"

"You put out."

"Nah, really why do you like me?"

"Well, geeze, look at you. We talked about past relationships some time ago remember?"

"Yes"

"What was the lacking quality about all of them? Whether it was your relationship or mine, what was it."

"I forget what is it?"

"What I like about you is the fact that you can form an opinion of your own and back it up no matter how much I disagree with it. This is what I really enjoy about you. I can hang out and talk about shit and argue and what not and in the end you and me can continue to disagree. I have met some women out there who actually believe that their opinion is not valid and that drives me crazy. I have argued with them and just when it was getting good they all of a sudden say okay you are right and they live with that. What a turn off."

"So you like me..."

"I like you cause you are a woman through and through, a woman with a fiery spirit and incredible kind heart. You have a sense of what you say is important no matter what others think of you. You feel about such things with a passion and earnest and say it with a smile, and then you can break down in tears over the frustration. You are more human than anyone that I have ever met."

"I do not know what to say about that."

"Ah, just say what on your mind, like I said you are good at that."

"Kiss me, you nut."

"I like that thought."

So I kissed her and then we sat back and watched the scenery zoom by us. Trains deserve to be a top ten destination for anyone. A fascinating

Chris Crase

piece of social thought went to the design and inception of the train system. The idea of amassing a cross section of the populous into a contraption to deliver us to our dreams all together. Were else can such a place be found in the world of fences, automobiles, suburbs. I sat there watching the world passing by under the Ka-chunk, Ka-chunk, Ka-chunk of its iron-laden tracks. Seeing the one lonely lamppost at a small town station, I saw I person we will call Bob get off and proceed to gather his things and walk down a deserted main street to who knows and just when Bob makes his choice on where to go my line of sight is cut off by the approaching buildings. Along through the fields where life resides in cricket chirps and owl hoots. We have life on the train. But what of Bob? Is he on his way to a long lost lover? A family? A mom and pop? None of the above? Where is Bob? Perhaps Bob just like Chris and I decided for life and just got off hoping to find a diner with a cup of coffee while he continues to examine this highway he has chosen. These shadows of Bobs all around the world appear before me in dreams at the wrong time of the night, every night. Were are all the Bobs going? Have these few proud folks found the answers we so long for and want to deserve. Am I just longing to have my shadow disappear with Chris' in the underlings of a street lamp of sun? To just be gone of this world and into one of new possibilities every night. Good luck Bob.

Never Fall in Love with a Vampire. It is a Pain in the Neck

Chapter 36

And thus that is when it happened for as soon as the train arrived in a town and we got off to start making our way back to our home, the lords had appeared in quite the numbers. It was a small town with little goings on there at the time of the night is was. Chris and I were strolling along into a park when they started to surround us. Chris grabbed my arm and looked at me. We both saw it in each others eyes that there was nothing to be done so with no resistance the lords took us and led the two of us silently entwined back to L.A.

Meanwhile, Morgan knew of the ambush and was hastily trying to locate the Prof. He scattered around the city looking for the places he thought the Prof would be. After no avail he decided to pay a visit to Marcus. Intelligence was pretty good for the lords and workers and we both knew very early in the tale where each other were residing. He arrived at Marcus' place and with maybe a moment of hesitation, Morgan walked to the front door and knocked. He waited there for all about a minute when he was clocked by some workers and was beaten bad as they dragged him into the home. The workers at once continued the hatred upon Morgan in the house. Morgan just took it putting up no fight except for the squirming of pain.

The commotion caused the emergence of Marcus, the Prof, and Timmy from a room. Seeing the display, the Prof and Timmy quickly turned themselves into the wolf and pounced onto Morgan's attackers throwing them from the death-friendly lord. The befuddled workers stood up and just watched as their comrades helped person from being killed. They all turned to Marcus for his reaction and all they got was leave them be. The Prof helped Morgan to his feet.

Timmy turned to Morgan and the others, "Marcus this is Morgan, yes he is a lord and is one of the few trying to help out Leif and Christine."

"Morgan, eh, well how is it that we can help you then." Marcus inquired.

Spitting out some dead blood and catching his breath, "First of all does anyone have a smoke, cause I really good use that right now."

The Prof fumbled in his cord jacket for his pack and gave one to Morgan.

Taking a drag, Morgan turned to the Prof, "Thanks"

Marcus growing impatient, "Now then Morgan what do you want?"

"It is Christine and Leif. The lords have them."

"What!" Timothy exclaimed.

Chris Crase

"Haden set out a group of us to track Christine. He threw her off by making it obvious to her that his servant was trying to trail her to let the others have an easier time. Anyway they have been, from what I gathered tonight, following her for days now and they planned to take them both."

"And you say they got them."

"Yes, they grabbed in a town up north from the rumors abounding. They are to be set on trial, as Haden puts it, tomorrow night. All the lords in town are suppose to be there."

"So you know where this trial is going to happen?" The Prof asked.

"Yes, about midnight at this warehouse"

"What is going to happen?" Timothy spoke.

"Knowing Haden and Marcus can probably back me up on this, Leif will die. As for what happens to Christine I do not know."

The Prof looking at Marcus, "We have to do something. We have to stop this once and for all."

Marcus moved away from the crowd to the sliding glass door overlooking the city lights. Deeply pondering the thoughts in his head he did not look outside just down at the carpet in front of him. All workers and lord stood idle in a fidgety silence.

"Nothing will be done." Marcus spoke.

"What!" Timothy, Morgan, and the Prof exclaimed in unison.

"The way I have figured it is this. Remember you who can the last time something like happened over Logan. We came in guns a smoking and for what? A lot of blood spilled, spirits broken, death... and for what? Logan still was killed nothing was done except driving into each of us and them a hatred for one another. If we do that again it will only drive the pain deeper and perhaps none of us will survive. No, this way is much better. Let the lords have their vengeance on Leif to spare the rest, that will cool their hearts and we can go back to the way things were before L.A."

"No." Morgan stood on his now.

"Pard me?" Marcus somewhat astonished and impress by Morgan's response.

"Leif is too good of a person to let this happen to him. I know that so does the Prof and his friends, Timmy, Jimmy, and Scotty. I even believe you know that. I am going to stop this because I have known Christine for a long time and I know this more than I have known a lot of things Christine needs Leif and Leif needs her."

"I will help." The Prof steps in.

"I too." Timmy speaks followed by Scotty and Jimmy.

Never Fall in Love with a Vampire. It is a Pain in the Neck

"What are you three going to accomplish? Nothing and probably be killed too." Marcus stopping the desention, "Morgan you are free to leave the rest of you come to your senses."

"I will help as well." Cloe steps into the mix.

"What!? Cloe you have despised Leif since I have had you keep tabs on him."

"Leif has a point though, this is about getting over a blood feud. Remember Marcus," Cloe pointing to her ears, "a door does not necessarily keep us from hearing."

"Damnit, then go and try to stop this if you will. It cannot be done, not now and not ever, there is to much anger, pain, memories for you and your band of rouges to suppress it." Marcus addressing Morgan and removing himself to another part of the room.

Morgan turns to the workers, "If you want to help Leif and Christine with the rest of us then come with me I know some people that can help."

And with that the band of rouges left by themselves.

Chris Crase

Chapter 37

So there I am sitting in a corner that I painted into. Chained to a pretty damn big column. I guess they thought I was stronger or something cause this column was massive. Luckily the chains allowed enough movement so I could get my smokes out of my pocket and enjoy a few before the firing squad. Morning was breaking through the windows of the warehouse that I was stuck in. The ware house was pretty nice looking as if it was built a year or too ago so I had the smallest of hopes that maybe some realtor would make his way through showing it off to some perspective clients and discover me. I wonder where Chris is?

I met Haden last night. He came in to size the catch of the lords. He seemed like a pompous snakeoil salesman. He did not say anything to me just conferred with the watch and the other lords. I just sat there, knees up and legs crossed with my hands atop. Some of the lords tried to harass me but I just sat there all kosher like. I just kept looking at the sky. From what I had over heard I had about one night left to go in this crazy mixed up world so there was no sense in being down. I just looked into the night air remembering all the good times and some of the bad times.

Now that it is morning I have the day to myself. All the guards and spectator have left. I sat there trying to keep my self busy with the cigarettes and not much else except my own muse. Wouldn't have guessed it. I figured out why my mulcher broke. I had forgotten to account for the amount of water rushing down the chambers. Overload. I wonder how Chris is sleeping. I hope they let her off easy, just seeing me die or something like that. She would get over that maybe in a few hundred years. A couple thousand years if I am egotistical. Yeah, a couple of thousand. Then again if I were the lords, I would not have her here and then just let her imagination run ramped with all the horrors they did to me. Now that would be cruel. Remind myself not to mention that idea to Haden and the others. I hope Chris is sleeping well. I wonder what they will do to me. Drawn and quartered? Drain all the blood from me? Maybe they will try that silver bullet thing I have heard about? Then again fire is not pleasant either. Maybe they will let Chris decide? Maybe they will have Chris do it? Now that would suck. Remind myself, not that idea either.

Thinking back on this whole thing it sound like a pretty trashy romance novel. I figured that this whole bit is cheesy. I could see the last few months of my life being sold at some supermarket checkout line. I wonder if they would get some good hunk of a man for the front cover and some sultry babe for Chris' character? Girls weeping at the pages wondering if old Leifer would be saved by some miraculous escape plan set up by his lover and his friends. Yep the people would read this two dollar novel wondering if they would ever have a love like Leif and Chris, if that would even be our names in the book. I do not think though that some knight in shining armor is coming. And as the pages of the romantic novel are read in the checkout lines of America the people would be wondering to themselves was it all worth it? Well was it? I would have to say yep.

Thus I carried on the rest of the day which was absolutely gorgeous. I would have liked to sit in a coffee shop today, one of those really low key dark and smoky ones. I hope Chris is sleeping well.

Chapter 38

Christine was bounded to a room at the hotel whereupon Haden and the council were staying. With daylight vastly approaching she could not dare to fight her way out as she was also being watched by some of the lords. The room was rather a bore considering it was in one of the most prestigious in the town. An arid smell floated through the air of the retro room with a large influence of Victorian age furniture. Christine described it as a horror show for anyone with a sense of any taste. Christine slumped into the chair and lit a smoke staring out of the westward window. Thinking of what might come of Leif and not really her cause the lords never harmed any of their kind before. Her imagination carried her into a torture prison beneath the streets of LA in the sewers. She saw a huge opening among the tunnels where Haden and his envoys were leisurely abusing Leif. Haden with his sketch pads drawing the wolfman in every manner not proud, just beat with no life left in his body. No glory left for her lover, friend, soul; nothing left but an even worse haggard body.

All Christine wished was for the ability to run to him and free themselves into a world that would forget them. She made herself over to the coffee pot and made herself some sludge.

"Christ," She mentioned to the room, "Can't even get a good cup of joe here."

She proceeded to pour out he the pot into an undersized mug that seems to be the trademark of all hotel rooms. Sunrise was coming and Christine had to pull the shades of the room shut. She moved the chair into the middle of the room and put the TV slash dresser in front of the window to cast a lovely shadow onto the chair and her.

"I hope Leif is resting." She thought to herself. "If anyone is letting him I pray that he can get some good rest. All I wanted was to be happy and now I had to fucking fall for a werewolf. Sure Christine you had no idea, then again you are very well at picking the ones that never work out. Maybe I should have just stayed with Morgan. Get a little home in the suburbs or something. Live the quiet normal life. Fuck what is the normal life, I am far far from it as it is. I mean I am the fairytales used to strike the fear into the population. The blood sucking mistress that can only feed upon the young pure male to sustain her life. The evil of mankind exemplified into a demon's soul of the human form. Quite ironic when one thinks of it. And to make life all the more normal I fall for what I even thought was a ridiculous myth. Who in the hell would of even thought of the man who can change into a wolf only to run off with your children while they tend to the

Never Fall in Love with a Vampire. It is a Pain in the Neck

family's livestock. I mean there is nothing really attractive about it when you think of it. When you think of it, think of it. Ah come on Christine stop with the thunk. I wish I could but I am wrong. It is my nature to suck the life from this world, and now all I want is to suck the life out of Leif, forever. Boy this coffee really sucks. I wonder why vampires are afraid of the sun? Maybe that is what it is a phobia maybe we can go out during the day then I could rescue Leif under the guise of day and escape up the coast for now and take off to never never land when the scene has cooled. Where is never never land?"

Christine got up and put another pot of coffee on and proceeded to the bathroom where she took a shower while the new brew brewed. As the warm waters fell over her and the steam lifted up into her lungs she still kept pondering the deal that had been dealt her. When she emerged from the shower, Christine was startled by the cleaning person making the turnovers in the room. Christine quickly threw her shrouded clothes on and made her way to the main room where the maid was just about to move back the TV slash dresser. Christine halted her and then proceeded to strike up a conversation with the young woman.

The woman looked to be in her young twenties with nothing really particular about her except her honest, innocent smile and excellent conversation skills. Her figure was quite normal for California with a healthy look of over exercising and under eating. The young woman, we will call her Ethel, turned out to be a mother of girl which one would never have guessed and a full time college student over at the university where Leif went to. It even turned out that she had a class with Leif. Among his regular studies Leif also enjoyed the undergraduate core classes which every student wishing to earn a piece a paper must subdue themselves to in the university life. Ethel did not know much about Leif except he was an antagonist in the class, especially when he was hung over which the TA absolutely hated. Among other things Ethel was quite naked about her life, she would say anything about anything concerning herself. Good or bad it did not matter. Caught up in Ethel's story, Christine offered her a cup of java and proceeded to keep the maid from continuing her services.

With a little nudging Christine had Ethel call the front desk and announce a fake illness to her employer and take the rest of the day off with Christine in her room. After that act was completed, Christine ordered some pizza and then really got frisky and order the most lavish drink from the hotel bar. The lords that were watching her from the next room even invited themselves over after hearing the ruckus. Soon the uptight security became fun as the food and spirits poured into the room, all on Haden's bill.

Chris Crase

Ethel and Christine began girl talk about lost romances and pitiful lovers; it was a full onslaught on the two male lords in the room. Ethel's story began with a high school sweetheart that broke her soul when he left for college. They had promised to stay together and when he returned after graduation they would marry and follow the path down which their parents had instilled in them. She heard the news about a month in the second semester of the freshman year. All in all good intentions fall apart when life strangles them. After that she was lonely and depressed for the rest of her school year as she was still in high school as a senior. Toward the end of the year she met someone just in time for prom and fooled herself into believing that this was her actual true love. This gent did not continue onto high education and instead stuck around working at his job which was pretty lucrative to an eighteen year old. They moved in with each other and the kid came nine months later followed by marriage a month later followed by the husband running away twelve months later with his new prom date. Ethel was over that by now and just trying to make amends with her life, but she always fell back upon her sweet memories of the sweetheart from earlier. Tricking herself into thinking that it was her one true shot at happiness. Or at least a more predictable life.

The conversation turned to Christine's love while the two males became nothing more than wall decorations for the last half hour. Figuring with nothing left to lose, Christine laid it all out on to Ethel's plate saving of course the fact that she is a vampire and Leif is a werewolf.

"So your, Uncle Haden is it has forbidden you to see this guy Leif and has you locked up in this room until he finds Leif and beats the hell out of him." Ethel recounted the story.

"You got it" Christine responded with the gaze of the two lords upon her for even bringing up the subject.

"What an asshole!" exclaimed Ethel, returning the glare back to the henchmen in the room. "And you two are helping this guy torment this girl" accusing the lords.

"It is not her place to decide" one of the lords responded to Ethel.

"It is not her place to live her own life." Ethel urged an argument.

"She made a decision and it was the wrong one. That is why Haden is here. To rectify the problem and return her and his life back to normal."

"But my life was the only one affected, Haden is just causing trouble cause of what Leif is and has no concern for my wellness." Christine interjected on her behalf.

"Not true, what about Jarred's life? His was most suddenly affected." The other lord whom was sitting quietly spoke up.

Never Fall in Love with a Vampire. It is a Pain in the Neck

"Who is Jarred?" Ethel inquisitively asked knowing there was more to the story.

"A friend of ours that Leif killed. That is why Haden is out for him."

"Leif killed your friend, Christine, you did not tell me that." Ethel exclaimed.

"Leif protected himself after Jarred attacked him without provocation and then proceeded to leave Leif for the dead." Christine corrected the lord. "Jarred had it coming after what he did to Leif."

"Jarred was only doing what he is expected to do when he encounters a worker like Leif, and we should expect the same from you."

"Hey! I did not even know he was a worker and if I did I still did not know what a worker was and upon all that it doesn't make any difference!" Christine pronounced upon Ethel and the lords.

"It does matter when it is a worker, Christine."

"Maybe to you."

"To all of us, and that is why you are here and tonight it will be all over."

"What is happening tonight?" Ethel inquired.

With that a lord accosted Ethel, the other held Christine back as she tried to interject to help Ethel. Within seconds Christine managed to free herself from the opposing force but alas Ethel's time ended just before. She laid upon the couch lifeless as the lord who took it from her.

Christine fell to knees in a lonely exasperation of defeat. She had enough… enough of everything. Her soul had been shattered into a thousand pieces with a sound of war burden children's cries. No tears wept form her eyes though only the silent motions of breathing as her mind processed all her emotion. Christine put her head into the palms as almost to try and place her thoughts into them and take away the pain. And with that the lords took themselves above her as a prophet or a priest looking for a baptismal or rather a born again baptismal.

One of them spoke, "Come Christine feed. You will need strength tonight."

"I would rather die."

"Do not deny yourself Christine, it is who we are."

"I have had enough of who we are."

"All will be better after tonight Christine. Soon enough you will forget this and Leif and all will be better you will see. So come now and feed."

Christine looked up at the lord with eyes of a child, looking straight through them at the pure souls of the men uncorrupted by the years of life. She rose and placed her hand on his cheek and continued her look for truth

Chris Crase

in him, with a tear forming in her eye she spoke, "You have really never known what it is to be alive have you?"

All he could do is stare blankly into her not making any sense of it all. The other lord went to the body and began to prepare it for its disposal, not at all interested in the situation.

Christine continued, "You I feel the worst for, even in some ways I feel more for you than Ethel there, at least she had something in her short life that you cannot even began to imagine. Tell me have you ever felt joy? Pleasure, save for your lust of blood? Fear? Anger, other than that for me and Leif? Love? Why do you continue to persist in this world if you cannot be apart of I?. When was the last time you let yourself to feel?"

Christine left her audience and went back to the chair and sat sluggishly into it. She grabbed a smoke still deep in thought; striking up the cig she began to smile and looked back at the steadfast lord.

"No, I do not think I will forget this." Christine said.

And with that the lord went to aid the other with removing Ethel form the room. They did not return and Christine waited for night to come in her chair.

Chapter 39

Night began to settle onto the city of wingless sullen angels. The bright inferno of millions and millions of years of ending energy was the only salvation for the two from the families of Capulet and Felatio. As the sun turned the ocean into a sea of silver slightly tarnished by golden reflections of lost sailors and wayfaring galleons as if to remind land faring souls that is not he the merciless unforgiving monster it turns into from time to time. Distance ships sounded their horns to announce the arrival of its husbands and wives to the ports of anxiously awaiting husbands and wives. And there is Christine, sitting in her jail among the stars of society. She waits for what her imagination is her only guide as has been yours in this tale.

Haden arrived into the stage and his group of lords. They gathered Christine without so much of a whimper form her. She just slouched around with them as they left down the hall to the elevator. Into the elevator they sped and out onto the first floor across the lobby. The entourage gathered in numbers in the lobby as a fleet of cars awaited them. Christine followed by Haden entered an enlarged SUV. The new model that just came out to battle the competitor's that just came out to outdo the others. This SUV was a towering seven inches longer with a two inch wider stance and a larger engine, towing capacity, overhead room, and cargo capacity. The interior of the Sport Utility Vehicle was standard among the class: leather interior, air conditioning, CD system, anti-theft device, heated chairs in all positions, no bench seats, of course four-wheel drive for the tough city streets, separate radio stations for all passengers, automatic transmission, a couple of thousand places for storing the knicks and the knacks, climate control for all passengers.

Haden and Christine were the only two in the back of the steroid limousine. Christine quickly lit a smoke felling a bit nervous as Haden instructed the driver. After finishing his direction toward the lord driving, Haden sat back, kicked a leg on top another and threw his arm around Christine's back rest. Haden's confidence made Christine choke on her smoke as she felt her stomach begin to tighten with Haden's gaiety.

"Alas young Christine, not to fret for soon we can put the pass behind us and look toward the future."

"It looks like the future is just more of the past." Christine muttered out.

"Yes, it may look that way and in a way it is but tonight we gain an upper hand in our struggle that began so long ago. We are sending a message out to our friends the workers that we will no longer tolerate our

Chris Crase

subversive manner to them. Your friend Leif will help us unite against the worker."

"And just what are you planning?"

"Ah, young Christine I am planning to set an example to the worker with young Leif about their rebellious and dangerous nature toward us, their lords."

"And you think that they will consider him an example or a martyr?"

"They might consider him as both, but it really does not matter for he is constituent to them and the effect will be the same. I am sure they will be angered at us and will perhaps be angered enough to try to strike back but it will be different this time because they will be motivated by the wrong reason, vengeance. From what I know of them this will die out and we will be cautious in our methodical removal of this nuisance so they shall dwindle and we will shall be rid of them for good."

"It would almost seem you would want them to strike back so you can wipe them out right now."

"Now Christine you are being optimistic." and a smile grew into Haden's face, "But they will vanish eventually and we will be alone with our way of life."

"Sounds pretty boring."

"Perhaps someday you will understand that this is the way it was and shall be. We are different from the worker, it has always been the way and we have had to deal with this past few years as an inconvenience but now we will not have to endure any longer."

And with that the two sat silently in the vehicle, Christine kept herself busy with cigarettes and matches. Haden just looked unto the scene as it passed along. A turn here and there, the stop signs made Christine prolong the agony longer as she sat quietly inside herself. Ever notice how stop lights make your trip exactly thirty seconds longer but it seems more like a good ten minutes? Anyhow the eventual destination came, it was a warehouse in the waterfront section of the metropolis. A plethora of cars were situated outside the in clusters of the tin walled building. The tin itself showed signs of corrosion and wear over the years including sea air, pollution, dirt, trash, vehicles, and of course man made wear and tear.

As Christine entered with Haden, the background reminded herself of one of those really weird cult movies with shrouded individuals in blackened monk robes. Torches were bearing insufficient light; in the center of the cement floor stood a cross of hardened steel, hey it is the 20th century. Other than that the lords made their way around the warehouse full of over enlarged crates. Some of the lords stood on the boxes while others crouched in their shadows still others were ascending up towards scaffolds

Never Fall in Love with a Vampire. It is a Pain in the Neck

for luxury box seats. Whispers surrounded Christine as Haden led her to her front row seat. The whispers were of that of a really bad day in high school where upon one could walk down the hall walls feeling the endless muttering and eyes glaring upon them for a different than "normal" walk, stride, haircut, book, or something.

Christine sat stood on the edge of a ring of people surrounding the cross when they brought me, Leif onto the stage for my final act. Two lords dragged me by the chains that bounded me and threw upon the center of the circle. I struggled to my feet and looked into the crowd for Christine. I spotted her and started to inch my way to her. I had been pretty badly beaten and all blood that was left in me was enough to sustain me for the next hour the rest was taken away in a not so pleasant manner. I really did not get the full assessment of my injuries until I saw Chris. She looked at me first with shock and a frighten chill as I would imagine sometimes the hunchback would receive; it was when she turned into a sigh gentle look of comfort to see me when I really understood how bad the wounds were.

"Hey Chris, how goes it?" smiling my bloody teeth at her.

"Ah, Leif." She returned my smile.

"No offense Chris, but you look like shit." lightening the mood.

"One should talk." she continued to smile back at me.

"Ah it is not all that bad."

"Could have fooled me."

"Come on Chris I mean I think I will turn this into the new look. I mean it seems to suit me well."

"I do not think it will go over well."

"Yeah maybe your are right. Well anyway what is a sexy looking women like yourself doing in this part of town?"

"Always making jokes aren't we, Leif?"

"Well ya know if you cannot laugh at one's self and situation you must be pretty uptight. Of course this probably isn't the best situation and tact should be considered but what the hell, I will not be around much longer might as well have a good time."

"Do not say that."

"Okay, I will try not to mention it."

"Ah, shit Leif, I am so sorry this has happened. I wish is wasn't this way, I wish we could have worked it out differently."

"Looking around Chris, I kinda wish it so myself."

"This is my fault, Leif, I should have stayed away. If I would have listened to them and stayed away you could have gotten away." Chris began to shed some tears.

"Hey Chris, I would not have let you stay away if you tried."

Chris Crase

"But we could have gotten away, we could have left."

"Why in the hell would we let them drive us away. Nah, this was a long time in coming."

"Well, it might be so but it still sucks." she stated as I brushed away a tear from her eye.

"Hey, Chris," spoken softly and confident, "Let me ask you this."

"What?"

"Would you have changed anything if you could? Cause I never would. You made me feel alive, something I have had in a long time."

"No, I believe I would not change anything either."

"You see then, no worries eh?"

"No worries." She smiled as she touched my cheek.

I started to make more conversation but the time had come as Haden directed the company to his attention. He stood in front of the cross in the center of the ring and had four lords grab me from Chris.

I did not make a struggle or a fight of it. Neither did Chris. I guess we just had exhausted too much to really try anything. Needless to say I did not help the lords, I just kinda made limp like an overworked piece of silly puddy. The lords took me to the cross as the crowd began to get excited with jeers and other gestures of ludeness. What is it that intoxicates a crowd into a frenzy like that over something so demeaning. Take for instance a man on death row taking his final steps toward the end of his life for the crimes he committed against the state and humanity. Crowds gather in multitudes to cheer the process of taking the soul of this criminal, cheering as the clock strikes midnight as if their consciences were being cleansed. We have chosen the answers and now our safety has returned and tax dollars freed from supporting a criminals life, in essence condoning his actions with theirs. Showing the rest that we are no better than the criminal just less taxed now. Then again it is probably not as cruel as keeping the person in prison for life to recount daily his guilt and maybe to find peace with themselves and life. Perhaps it is just easier to kill the criminal than to change the criminal. The people were so happy to see the suffering of another. Not unlike my predecessors I was drawn up onto a cross to see my final fate. First my wrists were tied to the cold steel, as the rope clutched around them I could feel the weight of my body on them. Next the lords took rope around my chest which helped alleviate some of the stress my wrists were enduring. Thus finally my legs were wrapped around the base of the cross this has always made no sense to me, I mean what am I going to do with my legs if they weren't tied, run away? Anyhow, after they finished, I looked like a makeshift Christ strewn out in front of the populous.

Never Fall in Love with a Vampire. It is a Pain in the Neck

Haden calmly let the crowd grow into a loud faceless mass of anger. He looked upon them as the lords put wood: cut for burning, around my feet. In my entire life I never would have thought to be burned at the stake. Then again it kinda fits my situation just like the witches of Salem. Burned for being different. I had to smirk at the irony. Haden made his way to the cross and carefully inspected the execution means. He looked at me briefly and I could tell that he was just buying time to let the crowd take the form that he wanted of impatient anger.

With one last trip around the cross he emerged on a tangent to the front of me looking at his brethren and directly at Chris.

Offering his alms, "Friends, we are joined here tonight night to pay retribution to our fallen Lord Jarred. Tonight we shall once again show our old enemies and workers who is top dog and the price that will be extracted to crimes committed against us."

Cheers cried out "For Lord Jarred! For Lord Jarred!"

Haden gestured to calm the chant and silence soon broke out. "However, my friends we have a slight new situation among us this time. It would seem that this filth that stands trial before us has fallen in love with one our own and once more this lord has returned his unrequited love. Now, how to deal with such an ordeal has plague us in the council. We have all heard her testimony that she indeed does not love this worker but there are some among us and even young Christine to believe this to be a lie. However, I do not believe this, after all he is nothing to us but a lad from a fallen class of people. We once provided for these people; saw after them; and then they betrayed us. Ever since then they have been after us to destroy our way of life and being in this world. And this lad, Leif, is no different. No, I do not believe that Christine was in love with him, instead I believe that she thought she had feelings for this worker and as some of us know Christine she has in the past been led astray by her feelings for people. An unwise heart if you will perhaps a result of prolong adolescence. For it is said that a young heart is often a foolish heart. And so my friends against the wishes of some council members I have decided to give Christine a reprieve in her punishment. She will not meet the same fate as her would be lover. Instead she shall live and live under strict supervision until the council seems fit to let her be. And not that she will not be punished if she continues on her ways, she will learn in time under my and the council's supervision. Young Christine shall learn to be a more conscience lord in matters of the heart and soul. For what lord could ever love or have feeling for anything other than our selves? After all are we not all of the same cloth and thus belong to each other. Christine will be brought into our love and

Chris Crase

understanding so that she may know us better and soon absolve her foolish ways."

The rustle of the crowd showed approval of Haden. However, the crowd angst to get on with the trial and so Haden quickly wrapped up his rap.

"Now, friends lets us begin." And the crowd fell silent as Haden motioned to some of the minor lords who quickly began to converge on me. Feeling kinda like a person backed in a corner as the flood approached, I nervously began to squirm. I looked up to see Christine and her eyes overflowed me with comfort. I began to smile at her and she returned the gesture. That was the last I saw before the lords overwhelmed my body.

At first the lords hovered around my crucifixion; I felt the air move around me as each one plotted their attack. One then ripped away my clothing next to my right thigh as another bit right through the back of shirt into my shoulder. Others joined in like a feeding frenzy of sharks and still others slashed my clothes and flesh to open wide wounds. Preference of their eating habits I guess. With each gash I felt my skin go numb until all the pain stopped. My bloodlines tried to heal and replenish the lost blood which only enticed the lords more and more. Every drop of blood that dropped was getting renewed, my body began to lose its battle with life. My soul began to lose touch with the world as I could feel it slowing down with each bite after bite. The light has dimmed.

Christine watched as my body fell limp idly by. Her eyes never left as the lords scavenged my body. The last thing I remembered was an incredible nose itch, of course the only place that seemed free of the slashing was my nose. Everything that occurred after this has been hearsay.

Never Fall in Love with a Vampire. It is a Pain in the Neck

Chapter 40

The crowd's chants echoed into the stank filled warehouse along with the clamoring of beating fists onto boxes and catwalks. The wounds on my carcass told the story well, 19 bite marks with 41 slashes for the wallet in my hand.

As the cheers died down to a calming satisfaction, Haden made his way over Leif's body. Examining the wounds upon the body, Haden seemed to be quite satisfied with the execution. He turned around to face Christine as a small smile grew into that of triumph. Christine did not look at Haden her eyes focused on the body in front of her. She smiled with ease as she saw her beloved finally freed from the torment. The spirit that was once so alive drew into her as memories of the past months entered her with joy. She could not help but smile in a satisfying pure love.

Haden saw this moment and in a glaring loss of understanding he motioned for the torches to burn the body. The lords swiftly gathered the torches and made there way to the thief on display. Without any hesitation they lit the kindling under the body as the crowd cheered. Christine did not move here eyes from the limp body as it was engulfed in a sunset of death.

The flames started to grow as it became hotter; inching closer to the flesh. And with each new flame that began a shout disappeared as the lords soon turned their attention to the walls of the warehouse. The tin of the walls amplified the bustling outside. Soon the only sound was the that of crackling wood. The sound grew and intensified to the main doors of the building. As all eyes were focused on the door; Haden made his way from the crowd to the front line of the lords.

The door opened to reveal Morgan standing alone. His eyes were focused on Haden alone among the other lords astonishment.

Haden spoke, "Morgan what is going on here?"

"I have here to end this." Morgan spoke.

"You have been corrupted by young Christine, haven't you?"

"On the contrary Christine has freed me."

"So it is your fate, do you think one man can stop this? No. I think your fate will be much unexpected."

"Not this time Haden, it is your fate that will be a surprise." Morgan spoke as he began to be joined by other lords. "You see Haden, I am not one man."

"Then such is fate of you shall fall upon this insurrection as well." Haden motioned to the faithful to deal with Morgan's handful.

Chris Crase

"Not so fast." A voice arose from the side of the building next to an entrance.

Haden a little annoyed now with the planned out but leading on play turned to the figure.

"Marcus?" Haden's voice turned from confidence to that of the unexpected.

Marcus stood at the doorway as workers made there way inside joining him by his side. Cloe, the Prof, Timothy, Jimmy, Scotty. All were present around Marcus.

"Haden." Marcus replied.

"Ah, Marcus" Haden's voice returning to a somewhat easy tone, "What have we here Marcus once again interfering in our business?"

"I have come for Leif, and I have also come to end this chapter in our two lives."

"Well I do not know what you have in store tonight but I can quite assure you that it will not end here, even if you have gained the liking of our lords. And as you can see you are to late for young Leif. We finished him like we did your sweet Sophia. He reminded me of you. Young and foolish, it was a shame that Logan had to interfere otherwise you could have been Leif here."

"Well Haden," Marcus unaffected by the remarks of the lord stood steadfast, "the way I figure it is that you and I have some unfinished business and we have managed to draw into it both of our peoples. Now I am here tonight because I am fed up with this course we are upon. So Haden, I wish to end it. Just you and me. Morgan and his friends as well as mine are here to ensure that it stays between us. Then after tonight what ever becomes of us we can hopefully allow our people to live their lives in mutually respect."

"We have no respect for you nor your kind Marcus."

"You may believe that and even some yours and mine would agree with you, and I cannot predict the future but I am here to end this hatred between us, so unless you have anything else I suggest we dismiss the pleasantries."

A grinned formed around Haden's eyes, "Friends!" he announced to the crowd. "It looks as if good fortune has sounded on us. After I rid us of the Marcus, deal with the rest."

Marcus disrobed and waved Cloe and the Prof over to pull down Leif's body as the flames began to engulf the young pup.

Christine ran over to assist them in cutting the ropes. Leif's body fell to the dirt; the Prof checked it for a pulse desperately. He looked at Christine's troubled face and tried to console her with his eyes, and then he looked at Marcus taking his glasses of and wiping his face.

"He is gone." the Prof said shaking his head trying to hide his pain. Marcus looked over to Haden awaiting. Haden smiled back at him. "He was more willing to go than old Logan." Haden spoke as all his hatred began to manifest in soul.

Marcus returned his hatred with a snarl that held years of repressed anger and frustration as he transformed himself into the wolf. As the two lunged at each other, the rest tried to engage in the melee. Small groups of workers and lords tried to go after each other but were thwarted by Morgan, the Prof, Tim, Cloe, Chris, and a handful of others. The handful soon grew and all eyes focused on the two enraging on center stage. It was if all of the emotions of the crowd fed the two spirits as the battle rose to that which rivaled the battle for Mt. Olympus. Gods began to tremble as the battle waged on, neither side gaining any advantage only more momentum as the crowd closely watched.

Marcus was able get an advantage as Haden let his guard down. A swipe from his claws tore away at Haden's midsection. Haden faltered back to regain his sense. Marcus pursued with death on his side; the wolf attacked again and again only to be repelled by the bat. Haden took to the air to maneuver around his foe more easily. Each bite that Marcus took with every swipe was only met with air. Haden's wound was bad, bleeding his black blood over the ground; however, Haden persisted and once the lunging of Marcus became a bit predictable Haden exploited the move and countered with a ferocious slap to the head of Marcus that open a wide gash onto his forehead running down to his snout.

Stunned and hurt, Marcus was blinded by his own blood. He hastily pawed at his face to regain the lost eye site but Haden took Marcus down to the earth and pinned Marcus under Haden's own weight. Marcus could feel the sweat of the vampire fall on his wound. Haden's breathing made the struggle all that much unbearable; Haden freed a hand to strike a blow to the side of Marcus' mane deranging the ear of the worker. Marcus let out a howl like the sails of a lost ship in the middle of a death ridden storm. Haden raised his head in a satisfying gasp bearing his fangs; the lord placed his hands over the neck of the wolf and forced it over to open an area next to the shoulder. He drove his teeth into the fur exposing the blood to his fangs.

The pain surrounded Marcus face as he could feel his life drawn out of him and into his long time hated friend. With every second Haden grew stronger as the pain left Marcus. Marcus' head fell back onto the ground and rolled over to see Leif's corpse and then onto the crowd behind his fellow worker. All the eyes were focused on him in a mesmerizing future. He saw in both lord and worker alike the fear of what is between their kinds. He saw Christine looking after Leif's remains, he saw Morgan looking at

Chris Crase

him with admiration, he saw Cloe looking on with fear, he saw the Prof shaking his head lightly, he saw twins concerned, he saw Jimmy concerned, he saw. And then in the glint of his eye he saw something else as he was barely hanging on. He saw my fingers move. And then he saw my forearm leave the dirt and reach for one of my more aching wounds.

Marcus turned his head to look at Haden with his eye. The glance was returned by the lord as they both saw the past in each other's pupil. They dilated to the present as each one grew weary of years that separated this moment. Then they became blinded by the future. Haden lifted his head and looked around at the crowd with a startled look on his face. The lord rose to the ground leaving Marcus on the earth exhausted. Wiping the blood on his mouth, Haden turned to the council. He removed himself from standing over Marcus and walked slowly over to them. His eyes were white as he looked to either side of the council at the mix of worker and lord in the crowd. He approached one of leaders and placed his right arm onto their shoulder.

"It is up to you now." Haden breathed slowly and then collapsed onto the ground exposing a hole in his chest through to his heart. The council member looked back at Marcus lying in the dirt with Haden's heart clenched in his blood soaked paw.

Cloe and Morgan ran over to Marcus and helped him to his feet. Once there, Marcus let the heart roll out of hand; he looked over the onlookers all still in stunned excitement. Cloe and Morgan tried to help him over to me as I was beginning to sit up. He looked at me and my wounds as I reciprocated sediment and gratitude. Shedding his support he walked slowly over Haden's body where the council made a crescent around the lying carcass. They all looked up from their fallen leader, and Marcus addressed the member that was touch by the hand of their fallen.

"It is over." Marcus spoke softly exhausted.

Never Fall in Love with a Vampire. It is a Pain in the Neck

Chapter 41

A couple of years later when I was just starting writing down these memoirs, I was visited by old Marcus. I was busy in Chris in mine's garden; you see we decided to settle down for a few years in the front range of Colorado. I was hell bent on trying to grow some sort of garden even as our lawns turned brown. It was during a long drawn out day in the August summer. I was in the middle of weeding or something I cannot quite remember when I noticed a figure walking up the earth driveway covered by the shadows of some pines. The figure had a small business hat on and old worn brown suite carrying a suitcase. I squinted my eyes to make out the figure as I was bent over a plant.

It was not until the figure was upon me that I recognized the scared face, old man. He was looking every so delightful while taking his handkerchief to wipe his sweaty brow. There with a smirk on his face and a step in his walk was Marcus.

"Marcus, what in the hell are you doing this far off the beaten path? Last I heard you were going over traveling the old land." I smiled standing up to extend my hand.

Taking my paw, "Well I was Leif but a little bird told me you had settled up here and I was on my way back to the Northwest for a while and I wanted to swing in."

"Ha!," a beaming grinned formed on my soul, "it is good to see you old man."

"You as well, friend."

"I hope that means you will stay for dinner."

"Absolutely, I ah, brought you a little house warming gift to christen your new home. It is not much." as he reached in his coat pocket.

"Ah shit Marcus, you need not have done that."

"Well, I was not very forgiving at our last meeting at I never had a chance to say sorry so anyway here it is." He revealed a garlic plant. "Besides the Prof told me you were attempting to start up a makeshift farm."

"Ha, thanks Marcus I will be sure to make this plant grow above all the others. I just came up with a new mix of fertilizer that can make anything grow in this climate." Laughing at the gift.

"I would love to here all about it over some ice tea."

"Oh shit, where are my manners come on lets get out of this heat and inside." As I gestured to Marcus to led the way up to the porch.

"By and by, Leif where is Christine?"

I looked at him kinda a weird, "Marcus she is sleeping."

Chris Crase

"Oh yes I forgot about that thing, how is she?"

"She is doing marvelous, she is considering teaching night school over at the local community center to help parents get their high school diplomas and also she is looking into taking in troubled teens into our home."

Heading up the stairs of the porch, "Geeze! I go on walkabout for a year or two and everything changes."

As our bodies entered the house and into the dark entrance way and the curtain begins to draw shut I responded, "Well as I keep on a saying 'you cannot stop the change.'"

The End

CPSIA information can be obtained at www.ICGtesting.com
Printed in the USA
LVOW04184710412

277209LV00003B/4/A